Off to a
Bad Tart

Jan Fields

Annie's®
AnniesFiction.com

Books in the Chocolate Shoppe Mysteries series

Library of Congress-in-Publication Data
Off to a Bad Tart / by Jan Fields
p. cm.
I. Title
                  2018938617

AnniesFiction.com
(800) 282-6643
Chocolate Shoppe Mysteries™
Series Creator: Shari Lohner
Series Editor: Elizabeth Morrissey
Cover Illustrator: Bonnie Leick

10 11 12 13 14 | Printed in South Korea | 9 8 7 6 5

Fall was in full swing in Moss Hollow, Georgia. Halloween had just passed, and scarecrows and jack-o'-lanterns had been replaced by more stately displays of bittersweet vines and uncarved gourds. The weather was about normal for autumn in the Peach State, and no one needed more than a thin jacket to be out and about during the day. The women gathered in the customer area of The Chocolate Shoppe Bakery wore lightweight sweaters and jeans, except for the few who hadn't changed from their church clothes.

It was Sunday afternoon, and the Southern Sweetie Pies, Moss Hollow's premier—and only—baking club were chatting and sharing treats. At one time, the Sweetie Pies had tried having the members host the meetings, but the logistics became too complicated. At Maudie Honeycutt's house, her husband, Hugh, blasted ball games from the den and made constant trips into the meeting for a bite of whatever luscious desserts the members had brought. In Josi Rosenschein's tiny kitchen, they'd practically had to sit in one another's laps. Cornelia Montgomery suggested they have all the meetings at Belle Haven since the mansion featured a formal dining room that was easily big enough for everyone and was rarely used, but then she'd started talking about the rules they would need to follow to placate the Belle Haven "haint" and the rest of the club had quickly lost interest in that particular venue.

As often happened with the Sweetie Pies, Bertie Harper had stepped in and settled everything. She'd offered The Chocolate Shoppe Bakery as the regular meeting spot. Settled in the middle of Main Street, the bakery was a practical choice, and no one made better coffee than Bertie. Everyone agreed, though Cornelia had sulked a little. She really felt the haint didn't get nearly enough attention, and she hated it when her twin sister made proclamations.

Although exceptions did occur, by the time Jillian Green returned home from California to help her grandmother, the bakery was well established as the usual location for Sweetie Pie meetings. Joining a group of such accomplished bakers often made Jillian feel a little inadequate—and the gossip featured her own life far too frequently—but she always looked forward to the treats.

The light from the bakery's front window glowed from behind Savannah Cantrell, Jillian's best friend, as she held out a tray piled high with chocolate cookies. "Want one?" Savannah asked. The cookies were dark, thick, and gave off a faint aroma somewhere between decadent and heavenly. Since Savannah was one of the best bakers in the club, no one doubted that the taste would live up to the aroma's promises. Jillian was always glad when it was Savannah's turn to bring in treats, and she reached out to snatch a cookie with a thankful smile.

"Savannah, dear, I am so jealous of your ability to bake and eat things like this so close to your wedding. With your fine figure, you don't have to worry about fitting into your dress," Maudie Honeycutt said, her bright eyes tracking Savannah like a coon dog on a hunt. The woman might resemble Peter Pan's grandmother, but she was as sharp as the captain's hook. "Which reminds me, you haven't shown us any pictures of your wedding gown yet."

Jillian smiled sympathetically at Savannah as she placed her cookie on the edge of her dessert plate to better admire it. The truth was that her friend had kept surprisingly mum at meetings about the plans for her upcoming wedding to James Wilson. Not that Jillian blamed her. The Sweetie Pies would take over in an instant if Savannah showed any sign of weakness, and before she knew it, she'd be draped in miles of satin and lace with the biggest hair in Georgia.

Fortunately, Savannah was anything but weak. She aimed a wink at Jillian before giving Maudie a sweet smile. "No, I haven't, have I?" She held the tray toward the older woman. "Cookie?"

Maudie gave Savannah a disapproving frown, but she took a cookie. "You are going to let us help, correct?" she asked.

"Of course," Savannah said. "You all know I'm counting on you to make the best desserts ever baked up for a wedding. But for right now, I have the other plans well in hand. I appreciate you wanting to help." She beamed at the club members. "I love all of you, but I'm not quite ready to be public with my choices. You can understand, surely. It's a bride's prerogative to be difficult every now and then."

It was clear from the expressions on most of the faces that the women could not understand. "We're worried that you might not have everything covered," Maudie said. "And we all have experience with this."

"I don't," Laura Lee Zane said brightly. Jillian saw the mischievous gleam in the eye of the young sheriff's deputy. "I don't know a thing about weddings, except that I'm certainly not having one anytime soon."

"Wise choice," Wanda Jean Maplewood said. Wanda Jean was Maudie's best friend and a coconspirator in most of Maudie's well-meant prying, but marriage was the one area where they disagreed. "I've been a widow for over twenty years now, and I still see no value in having a man clutter up a woman's life." She aimed a pointed gaze at Maudie. "And Hugh certainly comes with a lot of clutter."

Maudie tutted. "It's not so bad. I keep most of his sports memorabilia limited to his home office." She snorted a laugh. "Not that he does much work in there. Every time I walk in, he's mumbling and writing down numbers for his fantastical baseball league."

Laura Lee barked out a laugh. "I think that's fantasy baseball, not fantastical."

"Baseball might be more interesting if it was filled with fantastical creatures," Cornelia suggested. Jillian's great-aunt was an enthusiast for all things fantastical. Not only was Cornelia fully convinced that their house came with a haint, but she also believed that Bertie's cat, Possum, shared his body with the spirit of her late husband, Jillian's great-uncle Raymond.

Laura Lee giggled. "Bigfoot could be a power hitter."

Savannah offered the cookie tray to Laura Lee. "And all the zombies could play outfield since they can't run."

"Now that's silly," Bertie said. Jillian's grandmother wasn't a fan of silly. Though she and Cornelia were identical twins, they couldn't be more polarized in personality. While Cornelia was imaginative and eccentric, Bertie's feet were firmly on the ground, and that was where she liked them.

"Yes," Maudie said. "And distracting. We were talking about Savannah's wedding."

Savannah groaned.

Bertie pointed at her. "You stick to your guns, Savannah. If you want to handle your wedding planning on your own, you do it. It's your wedding. Have the one you want. But know we're here if you need us." Everyone uttered agreement on the last part.

Savannah reached into the pocket of her blazer and held up her phone. "I've got a planning book sitting at home and all my lists are in here. For now, I'm good. But I'm so grateful for how much you care."

"We love you. You know that," Bertie said gruffly. "And we can see how happy James makes you."

"He does." Savannah's eyes sparkled with joy.

Cornelia was sitting beside her sister and staring into her cup. She'd opted for tea over coffee, using a tea bag she'd pulled from her purse. She gazed at Savannah dolefully. "You need to be careful."

Savannah raised a quizzical eyebrow. "Careful of what?"

"I'm not sure. The tea leaves are unclear."

"Tea leaves?" Bertie's question was sharp as a knife. "What foolishness are you talking now?"

"My tea bag broke," Cornelia said, "so I've been reading the leaves. The meaning isn't completely clear, but it seems like a warning to me."

Bertie glanced over into Cornelia's cup. "It seems like a glop of wet tea leaves to me. Why didn't you use one of the tea bags we have here instead of something you've battered around in your purse for who knows how long?"

Cornelia ignored Bertie's whole rant, keeping her eyes on Savannah. "Something bad is going to happen. I see it in the leaves." She peered into the cup. "I see a gun and maybe a fish. I'm not sure."

"You see a glop," Bertie said firmly. "And I see an old woman with a vivid imagination."

Cornelia narrowed her eyes at her sister. "As I remember, you're two minutes older than me, Bertie Harper. I'm just trying to watch out for Savannah."

Savannah reached across the table and patted Cornelia's hand. "And I love you for it. I promise to watch out for guns and fish while I plan the wedding."

"You do whatever you want with your wedding," Bertie said, giving her sister one more annoyed glare. "As long as The Chocolate Shoppe Bakery makes your cake."

Savannah laughed. "That's a given."

"Yes, it is," Bertie said with a sniff. "And when you're ready, I have some ideas for the rehearsal dinner as well."

"I'll be all ears." Savannah nodded at the cookie in Jillian's hand. "Taste that already, Jillian. I want to know what you think. It's a new recipe I came up with. I thought I might include it in the classes we're doing through the Moss Hollow Parks Department."

"Yes ma'am," Jillian said. She took a bite of the cookie and hummed with delight. The cookie was almost as dense as a brownie, but with the interesting addition of butterscotch chips.

"I think her face says it all," Laura Lee said. "And I agree. This is a winner. You're giving out the recipe, right? I might want to bake some for the office."

Bertie raised her eyebrows. "You're taking goodies to work?"

"I'm trying to sweeten up Gooder. He's been a grouch lately."

Jillian harrumphed. Deputy Goodman "Gooder" Jones was a frequent thorn in her side. She'd known him since they were both kids, and they got along like siblings—in that he drove her crazy about half the time. But he was a solid lawman, and Jillian suspected Sheriff Coy Henderson had hopes of Gooder becoming sheriff someday. Granted, Sheriff Henderson wasn't about to retire anytime soon.

"I don't know about these cookies for the parks department class," Annalise Reed said. "Have you read the syllabus I passed out at the last meeting? It distinctly asks that we focus on healthy snacks."

"Exactly what every teenager longs for," Bertie muttered. "More healthy snacks."

Thanks to Bertie, some of Jillian's fondest childhood memories revolved around food, especially the items that would never be found on a healthy list. When she lived in California, Jillian had come to appreciate fresh, nutritious meals, but she loved comfort food as well. "It seems like we ought to be able to come up with a balance," she said. "Choices that are healthy with a dash of decadence here and there."

"I've read research that dark chocolate is quite good for you," Savannah said. She gestured toward the tray, which she'd set down on the table. "And with all the butter and eggs, this is practically a Southern breakfast food."

Annalise nibbled her cookie. "I'm not sure you'll convince Louisa Byrne of them being particularly healthful, but I definitely agree that they're yummy."

Jillian was beginning to wonder if Louisa Byrne was a figure created in Annalise's imagination. Despite her strict rules about class topics, they'd yet to meet the woman heading up a new parks department cooking class project, even though Annalise had talked about Louisa frequently when she'd introduced the idea to the Sweetie Pies of the group helping out with the program. Annalise had first met Louisa in the checkout line at Food for Less, and they'd struck up a conversation about how Moss Hollow High School had dropped their culinary classes due to budget cuts. Louisa had said that the parks department was trying to pick up the slack by having two cooking classes for teenagers, both meeting twice weekly. It produced a busy schedule for any teen taking both classes, but it allowed them to cover a variety of cooking techniques and skills. Several chefs from local restaurants would lead the more traditional cooking and restaurant skills class on Tuesday and Thursday nights. For Monday and Wednesday evenings, the mythical Louisa Byrne had talked to Annalise about possibly teaching a pastry class. Annalise had immediately suggested the club share the chore.

Since then, the Sweetie Pies had discussed who would lead the classes and, although Annalise seemed rather conveniently tied up on most Monday and Wednesday evenings, most other members had volunteered happily. They'd also gotten the syllabus. The one thing they hadn't gotten was a glimpse of the program director. Jillian brought that up. "Are we ever going to meet Ms.

Byrne? You keep talking about her, but it'd be nice to match a face to a name. And a set of rules."

"I'm glad you asked." Annalise turned toward the bakery door. "I believe this is her now."

Everyone followed Annalise's gaze as the door to the bakery opened. Since a large sign that said *Closed* hung on the front door, Bertie usually left it unlocked during the meetings to accommodate latecomers. No one in Moss Hollow would risk the wrath of Bertie Harper by ignoring her sign.

The athletic woman who stepped through the door had a swatch of sunburn across her nose and cheeks, which contrasted starkly with her otherwise fair skin. Her sunny blonde hair was pulled back in a ponytail, revealing multiple strands of gray near her face. She carried a denim jacket draped casually over her forearm, and her blue polo shirt showed off upper arms so toned that Jillian suddenly had the urge to do a few push-ups just to prove she could. The woman peered at the group through her wire-rimmed glasses and smiled. "I hope Annalise told you I was coming."

"Of course, Louisa," Annalise said, rushing over to greet the program director. "I was telling them that very thing just now." Annalise herded Louisa toward the tables. Although Annalise was certainly not an unhealthy weight, she appeared positively plump next to the fit program director.

"I'm sorry that I haven't made it to the last two meetings you invited me to," Louisa said. She shifted the jacket off her arm and onto a chair, and Jillian caught sight of a wide bandage near the woman's elbow.

Annalise gasped as she saw it as well. "Are you all right?"

Louisa glanced down at her arm and laughed lightly. "Yes, I'm fine. It's only cat scratches. My kitty found a mud puddle, and I had to give him a bath. He didn't like the idea."

Jillian remembered the last time they'd had to bathe Possum. He definitely hadn't been a fan of the process either.

"Cat scratches can get infected easily," Maudie said. "You'll want to watch that."

"I will." Louisa patted Annalise on the arm. "I want to thank Annalise for spearheading your involvement in this program, and I want to thank all of you for taking part. Cooking is an important skill, even for those teens not interested in a culinary career, so the parks department is happy to help fill that need."

"Do you have figures on the number of kids signed up?" Bertie asked. "According to the syllabus, the first class is tomorrow night, and we haven't gotten any numbers. That makes prep rather challenging."

Louisa seemed flustered by Bertie's disapproving tone, but she recovered smoothly. "Of course, and I'm so sorry for the delay." She launched into all the specifics that Jillian thought might have been helpful to know earlier.

Jillian leaned back in her chair and watched the program director. She found it interesting that Louisa had offered an apology but no explanation for why she hadn't attended any meetings previously. What had kept her from helping them organize what she seemed to think was such an important program? Luckily, Bertie had guessed at the number of kids pretty well, mostly by quizzing Celia Ryan, a teenager who worked afternoons at the bakery. The girl had attended several parks department programs, including a few led by Ms. Byrne, and knew the numbers to expect. Celia had also said most programs seemed well organized.

To a teenager, maybe. Jillian harrumphed inwardly. *Because the people they rope into teaching do the organizing.* She looked over at Savannah, who would be sharing the teaching with her on Monday. For the first few weeks, Savannah and Jillian would alternate teaching with Bertie and Lenora Ryan, Bertie's longtime right-hand woman at the bakery and Celia's father's cousin. After that, Maudie and Wanda Jean planned to take over Mondays, and Annalise said she was sure she'd be able to do a couple of Wednesdays with Laura Lee.

Savannah whispered to Jillian, "This is going to be so much fun!"

I'm glad one of us thinks so, Jillian thought. She had a bad feeling about it, and nothing about the program director was helping her shake it off.

Monday evening brought with it an early November cold snap, which for Georgia mostly meant that Jillian and Savannah were able to unload the boxes of cooking utensils and fresh fruit from the bakery van without sweating. Jillian definitely appreciated that since she was nervous enough without being sweaty too.

The Moss Hollow Community Center was a long, low, cinder-block building with all the character of a mud pie, though the community had tried to brighten it a bit about a dozen years earlier by adding cement planter boxes that were presently full of mums. The golds and oranges of the blossoms popped against the pale-gray building.

Other than the bakery van, there were only three other cars in the parking lot. Savannah had parked her cherry-red Buick Riviera in the far corner of the lot and was standing next to it, but Jillian didn't recognize the other two.

"I'm surprised you brought your fancy car," Jillian teased after she had parked the van next to Savannah's car and had gotten out. The recently fixed-up vintage automobile was quite rare and special.

"I have to take it out sometimes," Savannah said. "It's not good for a car to never go anywhere. They're like horses. They like to run now and then."

"I bet." Jillian's car, a little white Prius, wasn't exactly a racehorse, but Jillian loved it.

Changing the subject, Savannah said, "Too bad Louisa shot down my idea of teaching the girls to make those chocolate cookies. Nothing wins over a crowd like chocolate."

"I'm surprised you couldn't convince her of their health value. Your argument certainly won me over yesterday."

Savannah laughed as she followed Jillian to the rear of the van. "I should have brought charts or research reports. That's how I deal with stubborn clients. I drown them in information." Savannah was an accountant for most of the small businesses in Moss Hollow, which was an impressive feat. Jillian was competent with numbers, but couldn't imagine making a career from them.

"I supposed we should be grateful that Louisa agreed to fruit tarts," Jillian said as she opened the van door. She hefted a box of apples and handed it to Savannah, then slung a 25-pound bag of flour over her shoulder and grabbed a second box crammed with tools and jars of spices.

Savannah grunted under the weight of the apples. "I'll be more grateful when I can set this down. Chocolate cookie ingredients definitely weigh less."

Jillian shifted her own load, trying to get comfortable with the oversize box without letting the flour drop from her shoulder. "Maybe we can sneak chocolate cookies in later."

They started across the parking lot and Savannah managed a shrug despite the box she carried. "Maybe. At least making piecrust is a valuable skill."

"Right. I'm glad it's a skill *you* have." Jillian still struggled a little with her piecrusts. They tasted good enough, but she couldn't pull off rolling and shaping the perfect crust the effortless way her grandmother did. She wished they'd been able to shift piecrust to the next class, which Bertie would be leading.

Savannah glanced in her direction and smiled. "At least Bertie isn't here making us wear hairnets." Like Jillian, she'd pulled her shoulder-length brown hair back into a ponytail, though Savannah's ponytail was sleek and shiny, while Jillian suspected her wild red curls made hers look more like a clown wig.

They carried the boxes into the community center. Near a reception desk was a sign that said *Teen Baking Class, Room 12.* They walked down a hallway and found the door marked *12.* Inside, Jillian spotted two teens she didn't know dragging stacked chairs noisily across the floor toward rows of tables. Louisa Byrne stood at the front of the room, laying out papers on one of the tables. "Jillian! Savannah! I'm glad to see you. Is this arrangement all right?"

Jillian examined the rows of tables. "Seems fine to me. As long as everyone has enough space to work. We'll need to sanitize all the tabletops if we're going to roll out dough on them."

"No problem," Louisa said cheerfully. "Bertie told me yesterday that all the surfaces had to be sanitized. She also recommended muslin stretched over the tables to make cleanup easier." She gestured toward a roll of cloth. "The fabric shop donated a roll, and I brought plenty of clips to hold it down."

"And I see you brought assistants of your own." Savannah set her apple box on the front table and gestured toward the teens.

"I roped in help from the tennis class I teach. This is Avery Morgan, and this is Faith Griffiths."

Avery came over and peered into the box. "Apples? Are we making applesauce?" She wrinkled her nose. "We eat a lot of applesauce at school."

"No applesauce," Jillian said. "We're doing apple tarts."

"Tarts?" Faith walked over as she pulled her long black hair into a messy ponytail. "Is that like pie?"

"It's very similar to pie," Savannah said, and both girls cheered until Louisa thrust bottles of sanitizer and clean rags at them.

"Those tarts better be good," Avery said, making a face, "because I'm really working up an appetite."

"That's the wonderful thing about this program," Louisa said. "They'll be as good as you make them."

Faith nudged Avery with her shoulder as she took a bottle of sanitizer. "In that case, you're doomed."

"Ha, ha," Avery said flatly.

Louisa clapped her hands. "Enough chatting. We still have plenty more to do before everyone arrives."

Despite Avery's complaints, Jillian had to admit that both teenagers tackled the job of sanitizing the tables with gusto. The surfaces were soon squeaky clean and covered with crisp muslin held to each table with plastic clamps that were designed to hold vinyl cloths on picnic tables. After a few more trips to the van for supplies, Jillian and Savannah worked on setting up their workstation at the front of the room. As they did, more teenagers drifted in, including several boys, which Jillian was pleased to see. When she was a teen, few of the boys at school would get anywhere near anything relating to cooking.

Jillian recognized the last two teens to shuffle in: Celia, whom she knew well from her after-school work at The Chocolate Shoppe, and Celia's friend Sidney. Jillian had met Sidney when she got into trouble because of a creative and unfortunate choice of school project. At the time, Celia and Sidney had also toyed with the idea of being amateur sleuths, but Jillian was pretty sure they'd lost the taste for that when their adventure had nearly got them killed.

"Hi girls," Jillian said. "I didn't know you were taking this class."

Celia started to answer, but she was interrupted when Louisa clapped her hands again to draw attention to the front of the room. She introduced the program in cheery tones and seemed unaware of the expressions on the faces of the audience. "Though this is a pastry class," the program director said, "we're going to focus on healthier snacks and desserts. Treats don't always have to be bad for you."

Jillian almost giggled at the students' groans and eye rolling.

After Louisa turned the class over to them, Savannah stepped up to begin. "Tonight, we'll be making apple tarts," she said. "Tarts, like pies, are a marriage between two different elements that don't always play well together. Wet fillings can lead to soggy crusts, but no one wants a completely dry tart either. So you've got to have balance."

Jillian admired her friend's ease in front of the group of teenagers. She also noticed they were paying much sharper attention to Savannah than they had to the program director. She glanced in Louisa's direction and saw the woman gathering her things. Jillian sidled over. "You're leaving?" she whispered.

"Yes, I have to get home."

Jillian grinned at her. "More cat washing?"

"What?" Louisa looked at her blankly.

Jillian pointed at the bandage on Louisa's arm. "The bath disaster."

Louisa stared at the bandage for a moment, then offered Jillian a tight smile. "Right. No, I am definitely avoiding any more disasters."

Something in Louisa's tone made Jillian peer at her closely, but Louisa avoided eye contact and kept shoving things into her tote bag. "The girls know where everything goes. They'll help you clean up the room after class."

"That's—" Before Jillian could say more, Louisa hurried out the door.

Jillian returned to the front of the classroom, hanging off to the side while Savannah explained the importance of cold butter to a good crust. She handed Jillian a bowl filled with sticks of butter nestled in ice. Each stick had been cut into pieces the correct size for a single tart crust.

"As Jillian comes around, each of you take one chunk of butter," Savannah instructed, "but handle it as little as possible."

Jillian carried the bowl to each table, wondering if Bertie would be disappointed in her for taking a back seat in the tart crust instruction. It wasn't like she *couldn't* make crust. She had made her fair share for the bakery, but she usually left crusts to Bertie or Lenora, who had more experience and more of a knack for them.

Savannah smiled as Jillian returned to the front. "As soon as we finish this crust, Jillian will show you how to make the filling," she said.

"I will?" Jillian asked, eyebrows shooting up. The surprise in her voice made the teens giggle. She could definitely make filling, but doing it with an audience was a daunting endeavor.

"You'll do fine," Savannah whispered, though obviously loud enough for the first row to hear, since they snickered.

Photocopies of the tart recipe had been handed out at the start of class, and Jillian picked up a leftover copy to study. The filling was straightforward. *I can do this.*

As Savannah demonstrated cutting the cold butter into the flour, Jillian crammed for her part, mentally walking through the steps. She heard the heavy door to the room open and looked up, wondering if one of the teens was late for class. To her surprise, Louisa slipped through the door. The woman's complexion was ashen, and she dropped into a chair near the door, clutching her tote bag to her chest.

Jillian glanced at Savannah and estimated how much longer she would be focused on dough. Figuring she had a few minutes, she slipped over to the door. "Are you all right, Louisa? Did something happen outside?"

Louisa gazed at her without speaking for a moment. She forced a smile that looked like a tight slash across her pale face. "I'm fine." Her voice shook, and she paused and swallowed. When she spoke again, her voice was steadier. "My evening appointment was canceled, so I can stay and enjoy the class. I've always struggled a little with piecrusts myself."

"Me too." Jillian continued to study the other woman. Clearly she was lying. Something other than a canceled appointment was affecting her, but Jillian was in no position to get the truth out of her. It really wasn't any of her business.

Jillian turned back to see Savannah gently pressing dough into the tart pan. With a last curious glance at Louisa, she hustled back to the front table.

Savannah was wrapping up her instructions. "As soon as your shells are ready, line up your pans on the back counter near the oven," she told the teens. "I'll blind-bake your tart shells while Jillian helps you with the filling."

"Why do you have to be blind?" one of the teenage boys asked. "Is this like some kind of competition?"

Savannah smiled at him. "No, sorry. 'Blind-baking' is a pastry term. It means to bake your pie shell before you put in the filling. Before we do that, though, we have one last step to prepare the crust: docking." She grinned. "Which is another pastry term that means 'poke it a bunch of times with a fork.'"

As the teens gleefully stabbed their tart shells, Jillian glanced toward Louisa. Although her skin had resumed its normal coloring, she was clearly far from relaxed, frequently stealing peeks at the closed door. Before Jillian could give in to the urge to go talk to Louisa again, Savannah waved her over. "As soon as you have docked your crust, come and line up at the counter. I'll need to mark your pans so we get the right crust back to the right person." She leaned close to Jillian and whispered, "Good luck."

"Thanks." Jillian watched the group carry their tart shells to the oven, each cradling the crust as if it might leap out of the pan if not held completely steady. She liked seeing the pride on their faces. They might give in to the occasional eye roll, but these kids were clearly enjoying this. That boosted her own spirits a bit.

When all the teens were back at their tables, Jillian tried

to radiate the same confidence she'd seen from Savannah. "The perfect tart filling balances sugar and spice. And it all begins with your apples." She held up an apple from the bowl. "You'll notice these don't come peeled and cut up, though those are both important steps." She held up a vegetable peeler. "Now, my grandmother can peel an apple perfectly with a dull knife, but I like a vegetable peeler. I do a lot less bleeding that way." To her delight, the teens laughed and didn't roll their eyes. *I might be okay after all.*

She walked them through preparing the apples and tossing them with lemon juice to keep their color. Then she started on the glaze that would be poured over them. "In a two-crust pie, you mix the apples and glaze together because no one is going to see them. But in an open tart, the apples are on display, so we'll be making an arrangement with them."

"What if I'm not artistic?" one girl asked. "My slices aren't very pretty."

"Baking is art," Jillian said, echoing something Cornelia had told her to lift her spirits during her early baking fiascos. "Imperfections are part of what lets the consumer know it was made by hand. We're not making tarts on an assembly line. Each one is supposed to be different." Then she grinned at the girl. "If it ends up looking really unique, we call it 'rustic.'"

"Mine is going to be *so* rustic," the girl said, and several others agreed.

The preparation of the filling went smoothly, and Savannah carried the baked shells back to each table. Jillian walked them through arranging the apples in a spiral in the bottom of the crust and pouring the glaze over it.

"This smells so good," Sidney said. "It's making my stomach growl."

"Oh, that's your stomach," Celia teased. "I thought we were

being attacked by wolves." Her friend elbowed her in the ribs and laughed.

"I love the smell of the spices too," Savannah agreed. "To me, an apple tart smells like autumn."

The rest of the lesson went well, and they managed to get all the tarts baked without any catastrophes. Granted, Jillian noticed more than one of the teens seemed to be wearing a lot of flour and cinnamon, but that was all part of the fun of baking. As the tarts came out of the oven, the aroma filling the air was heavenly.

The door to the room banged open. Louisa jumped out of her chair, dropping her bag and spilling the contents across the floor. Savannah hurried over to help Louisa gather her things, but the other woman shooed her away, her wide eyes darting toward the newcomer in the doorway.

The man who entered was tall and broad-shouldered, with a head of short dark curls. "I hope you saved me some of whatever that is you're making, Celia," he called out. "I got hungry just walking across the parking lot."

The gleam in the man's eye was instantly familiar to Jillian. There was a strong resemblance between him and Celia, and Jillian knew in an instant that this was her father, though she hadn't met him before.

"Of course I did, Dad," Celia said. "And I have the recipe. I can make more."

"Good," he boomed. "You tell your mama we're having that for Thanksgiving dessert."

Jillian walked over and offered the man her hand. "Mr. Ryan, I am pleased to meet you. I'm Jillian Green. We'd be lost without Celia's help at the bakery."

The big man gazed down at her speculatively. "Call me Anthony. Celia speaks highly of you, though my wife's sister Jasmine says you're nosy as they come."

Considering the help Jillian had been to Jasmine Jackson when her salon, the Clip & Curl, had nearly burned down, Jillian was mildly miffed by the remark, though she knew Jasmine well enough to know she probably had something snarky to say about every citizen in Moss Hollow. Jasmine was full of strong opinions and sass, but she also had a loving heart. "I have my moments," Jillian said mildly.

Anthony laughed and engulfed Jillian's hand with his, shaking it was surprisingly gentleness. "Don't we all?" He turned to his daughter. "Gather up your stuff, kiddo. Time to go."

"Don't forget we're giving Sidney a ride home," Celia told him.

"Then have her get her stuff together too," Anthony said, flapping a hand at her. The girls gathered their belongings at the glacial speed that only teens can manage. He gazed at them and shook his head. "I'll wait in the truck."

As he walked back out the door, Jillian looked at Louisa, who had finished gathering her belongings and stood leaning against the wall, her gaze still on the door. Something had the program director scared. But what could it be?

Sidney and Celia managed to drag out their packing up until they were among the last to leave, even chipping in to help stack chairs and fold up tables.

"Shouldn't you two get outside?" Jillian asked. "Your father is waiting on you."

Celia shrugged. "He doesn't mind. He's used to us."

Louisa rallied enough to help set the room in order, though her cheer was too brittle to fool anyone. Jillian saw that while Louisa kept her eye on the door, Celia and Sidney seemed to be keeping theirs on Louisa. She wondered what was up with the two teenagers, but she knew she'd probably only hear what was on their minds when they were good and ready to share.

Savannah tucked the spare disposable tart pans into a box of supplies. "Since you have so much help, do you mind if I take off? I hate to leave you with work to do, but I promised James I would meet him." She dropped her voice to a whisper. "We're working out some wedding details."

"Of course, go ahead. But you know you're driving the Sweetie Pies crazy by keeping them out of the loop. I'm doing my best not to let anything slip, but it's a challenge to say the least."

Savannah sighed. "I know, and I'm not doing it to be mean, but you have to admit we have some, ah, forceful personalities in the club. I want to be sure my wedding stays mine, you know? I figure if I have all the details in place before I give specifics, there's a better chance of that happening."

"You don't have to explain it to me. Remember, I live with Bertie Harper and Cornelia Montgomery. I know all about forceful personalities." Jillian made a shooing gesture toward Savannah. "Go on. The apple box and flour bag are much lighter now. I'll be fine."

"No argument from me. See you on Sunday, if not earlier."

As soon as Savannah left, Louisa appeared at Jillian's elbow. "May I help you carry some things to your car?" She had her own tote bag over her arm and was offering Jillian the same brittle smile she'd worn for half the night.

"That would be nice." Jillian put the partial sack of flour into the apple box with the few remaining apples and handed the crate to Louisa, then she grabbed the other box. "I came in the bakery van, so you can't miss it."

The teens finished shoving the last of the chairs into the storage closet, and Jillian and Louisa followed them out of the room. Celia, Sidney, and a couple of other kids lingered outside the classroom, chatting and laughing, but Jillian and Louisa continued down the hall to the exit doors. Jillian watched the program director as they crossed the parking lot. Louisa froze when the driver's-side door of a big navy-blue truck in the lot swung open. She visibly relaxed as Celia's dad leaned out. "That daughter of mine coming?"

"She'll be right out," Jillian called to him. "They just finished cleaning up."

Anthony grumbled something in reply and closed the truck's door.

"Are you worried about something?" Jillian asked Louisa as they finished the walk to the van.

"Worried?" Louisa echoed.

"You jumped every time there was a loud noise in the community center, you nearly passed out when Celia's dad opened his truck door just now, and when you came back in from the parking lot, you were whiter than the flour in the pastry."

"I'm sure you're exaggerating."

"Not much. If something happened when you tried to leave earlier, you should tell someone."

Louisa forced the fake smile back on her face. "I heard some rustling in the brush." She pointed toward the edge of the parking lot. The community center backed up to some unused land that mostly harbored poison ivy and briars. "And something growled. I didn't want anyone to know I was being so silly over an animal. After all, there is a lot of wildlife around here."

"Something growled?" Jillian asked, peering toward the brush. "Maybe a stray dog? We don't have a lot of growling wildlife."

"I know. I'm being silly. I got spooked in an empty parking lot. Don't tell anyone, okay?"

Jillian still wasn't sure about Louisa's story, but the last part sounded sincere, so she said, "No problem. We all get spooked sometimes."

At the van, they loaded the boxes quickly. Louisa gave Jillian another tight smile and thanked her. Jillian wondered if the thanks was for helping with the class or agreeing to keep her secret. She nodded in reply, and Louisa hurried over to her car.

Jillian watched, bemused, as Louisa peeled out of the parking lot.

"Did you find out why she's acting so weird?"

Jillian faced Celia and Sidney. Ignoring Celia's question, she said, "Your dad is getting impatient. Thanks for staying to help, but you two best go on."

"Oh, come on," Celia moaned. "Don't be one of *those* adults."

"One of what adults?" Jillian asked.

"The kind who doesn't tell us anything because we're kids," Sidney chimed in. "Which we're not. We're plenty old enough to see that Ms. Byrne wasn't being her normal self. Something is going on. Did you find out what?"

"Yeah, you had plenty of time to question her," Celia said. "Did she spill?"

"Spill?"

"Confess," Sidney said. "Unburden herself."

"Why are you two acting so strangely?" Jillian asked, narrowing her eyes at the eager teens.

Celia crossed her arms over her chest. "You aren't the only one who can figure things out. Sidney and I have noticed Ms. Byrne acting twitchy for weeks. Something is up with her, and we're going to get to the bottom of it."

"That sounds like an invasion of privacy," Jillian said.

Celia snorted. "Like you worry about that when you're poking into other people's business. You're jealous because you're not the only detective in Moss Hollow anymore."

Jillian gaped at the teenager for a moment, too stunned to respond. "I'm not a detective," she finally managed. "And neither are you."

Sidney winked at her. "Sure, right. Now the big question is, do you want to be kept in the loop when we discover her big secret?"

Jillian groaned. There was clearly no heading this off. "What makes you think there is something wrong with Louisa Byrne? Is she not normally a nervous person?"

"She didn't used to be," Celia said. She and Sidney exchanged glances. "She's been with the parks department for about a year, so we've been in a ton of her programs."

"By 'a ton of,' she means 'four,'" Sidney said.

"The important thing is that she was totally chill during most of the spring and summer programs," Celia said forcefully, clearly miffed at Sidney's correction.

"It was impressive, the way she could be calm, considering the whole thing about her husband," Sidney said.

Jillian raised an eyebrow. "What thing?"

Sidney and Celia stared at her in wide-eyed surprise. "You didn't know?" Celia asked. "Her husband was a big-time crook. He's in prison."

Jillian felt a pang of conscience. She knew how it felt to be involved with someone who was a "big-time crook." Her former fiancé in California had embezzled from the company where he worked and had ended up in prison. The gossip had followed Jillian everywhere, along with questions of how much she had known about his activities. The answer was nothing at all, but that didn't slow down the rumor mill, and it had eventually cost her her job.

She leveled her gaze at the two eager teens. Not only was she gossiping about this woman's horrible experience, she was doing it with children. "Ms. Byrne has a right to her privacy. If something is bothering her and she needs help, she'll go to someone she trusts. And that's not likely to be a bunch of nosy busybodies outside a community center."

Though Celia was clearly annoyed by Jillian's rebuke, Sidney hung her head guiltily. "We only wanted to help," she muttered.

"And I'm sure Ms. Byrne will let you know if she wants your help."

At that moment, a deep voice bellowed, "Celia Ryan, you get in this truck right now, or I'm leaving both of you and you can walk home in the dark!"

"Yikes, he sounds mad," Sidney said.

Celia gestured dismissively. "He's all bark and no bite."

"Let's not test that theory. I don't feel like walking." Sidney grabbed Celia's arm and pulled her toward the truck. Jillian watched them leave, hoping she'd convinced the girls to drop their sleuthing.

The next two days were busy at the bakery, though Jillian had trouble remembering the last time the bakery had been anything but busy. Worried about how hard her grandmother was working, she made sure to get up in time to drive in early with Bertie every morning. One of these days, Jillian was going to get up the nerve to broach the subject of Bertie's retirement, or at least of her taking more days off during the week, but she hadn't quite gotten that brave yet.

On Thursday morning, the day after Bertie and Lenora had taught the second parks department class, Jillian insisted on coming in early so Bertie could sleep in. "I know how tiring those classes can be," she insisted and was surprised when her grandmother didn't argue at all.

She'd gotten all the yeast breads measured into the huge mixing bowls when Lenora came downstairs from the overhead apartment to join her. Lenora had been working at the bakery as long as Jillian could remember, and she felt like family—and often nagged Jillian like family as well.

"Sorry I'm late," Lenora said as she pulled a pink hairnet over her close-cut graying curls. "I never sleep in. I don't know what got into me. Where's Bertie?"

"She slept in too," Jillian said. "I only saw her briefly last night when she got back from the class, but she looked beat. Did the teens give you a hard time?"

"Not at all." Lenora walked over and flipped on the first mixer. The huge bread hook rotated in the bowl, plowing through the flour, honey, warm water, eggs, and yeast. "Those kids were great. They are so excited about baking. It's nice to see that in young people."

"How was Louisa? Did she seem to be acting strange?"

"Strange how?" Lenora asked. "She seems like a high-strung sort, but she clearly enjoyed the class as much as the teens. She stayed all the way to the end and even helped carry stuff out to the van. You can't ask for more dedication than that."

"But doesn't that seem odd? Did she seem afraid to go outside without you?"

Lenora put her hands on her ample hips. "What are you up to, Jillian Green? You know Bertie would say you imagine a mystery behind every bush."

Jillian held up her hands. "I know, I know. It's just that Celia and Sidney thought her nervous behavior was weird."

"So now you're taking advice from teenagers?" Lenora asked. "I love Celia like my own young'un, but that child has more than her share of imagination. She's always prowling for some way to make life more interesting. Don't get caught up in that—you'll only encourage them."

"Fine," Jillian said. "I just wanted to know about the woman's behavior."

A familiar voice spoke from behind her. "If you want to pay attention to someone, it ought to be Hunter Greyson." Bertie bustled into view, tying on an apron. "After all, Savannah is getting married. Surely you don't want to be the last spinster in Moss Hollow."

Jillian groaned. "Hunter is perfectly happy with the amount of attention he gets." Her relationship with Hunter had built slowly, but Jillian felt like they were in a good place. "And no one says 'spinster' anymore."

"Well, I said it." Bertie grabbed the order clipboard from the table next to Jillian and stomped off toward the front of the shop to put the coffee on before they opened for customers. "And you best get on those bear claws."

"They're already in the oven," Jillian called as her grandmother left the kitchen.

As soon as Bertie was gone, Lenora chuckled. "I reckon Bertie done told you, spinster girl. Not that I don't agree that your time is better spent focusing on your boyfriend. Hunter is surely someone worth studying."

Jillian stared at the doorway, annoyance battling with curiosity.

She wasn't interested in any more nagging about Hunter, but she suspected Bertie would know all about Louisa's ex-husband and whatever he'd done to land in prison. There wasn't much gossip that didn't pass through the bakery. Jillian decided she didn't have the energy to butt heads, so she switched on the second mixer. Maybe she'd try to get the truth from Bertie later.

As usually happened, the heavy workload made the morning pass quickly. After finishing with the bread orders, Jillian moved on to a batch of pumpkin pies. She started with the pie shells. If a room full of teenagers could tackle a piecrust successfully, it was high time she overcame her own crust phobia.

She was weighing flour for the batch when Maggie, the bakery's countergirl, ducked into the kitchen. "Can I take a quick break to run to the drugstore?" she asked. "I need to pick up a prescription for my grandmother. She's sick, and I want to run it by her house during my lunch break."

"You go on," Bertie said. "And once you get it, take it right over to Elizabeth. I know how stubborn that woman can be, so if she's sick enough to admit to needing medicine, she probably needs it right away."

"That's kind of how I felt," Maggie said. "Thanks. I'll get the line down a little, then dash out. I'll be back as quick as I can."

Maggie ducked back into the customer area. Jillian expected Bertie to go out front and wait on customers, but instead she shooed Jillian away from the work area. "I'll work on the pies. You go wait on customers."

Out front, Maggie was handing a white paper bag to a tiny woman in line. Jillian recognized the elderly woman immediately and flinched. It was Ophelia Jones, the only woman in Moss Hollow scarier than Bertie. She didn't like Jillian at all, and she usually had plenty to say about the matter. "One lemon-poppy seed muffin," Maggie sang out. "Fresh this morning."

"Thank you," Ophelia said, then she caught sight of Jillian. Jillian was sure she was about to catch a diatribe from the woman, but Ophelia only sniffed and spun on her heel, marching out of the bakery with her bag in hand.

Must be my lucky day, Jillian thought as she took over for Maggie. She was surprised to see Stewie Franks still in his usual seat and perusing the newspaper. Normally he'd be done and gone by so late in the morning. *I guess everyone got a late start today.*

Maggie left on her errand, and Jillian steadily shoveled bear claws and muffins into bags and poured cups of coffee for the seemingly never-ending line of customers. For every person who left, someone new walked in. Jillian was grateful that the bakery was busy, but she was also glad she didn't always work the front.

She watched two chatting customers leave as another came through the door. To her surprise, this one wasn't familiar at all. By now, there weren't many people in Moss Hollow that Jillian hadn't met or at least seen in passing. But she knew that she'd never laid eyes on the tall, attractive man who strode over to peer at the selection of baked goods in the glass display case. Apparently she wasn't the only one who noticed the stranger, as she saw eyes turn toward him from all over the bakery.

Eventually, he ambled to the line and, when he'd reached the front, Jillian smiled up at him. "What can I get you today?"

"That smile alone is right nice," the stranger said.

"But it probably won't fill your stomach," Jillian replied, brushing off the faint whiff of flirtation. She gestured to the cases. "Did you see anything you like?"

"Nothing I like as much as what I see now."

Jillian's smile slipped. She could see the other customers' interest was piqued by the man's flirting, and she did not want this to become fuel for the gossip mill. "If you aren't interested in buying anything, perhaps you could let the next person in line step up."

"Aw, that hurts." The man mimed a blow to the heart. "But if you insist. What do you recommend?"

"The bear claws are popular," Jillian said.

"I'll have one of those then, and a bit of information if it isn't any trouble."

Jillian tensed, hoping against hope that the man didn't ask for her phone number or do anything else to feed the interest of those around him. She already suspected it wouldn't be long before talk of this encounter got back to Hunter. Although she knew he'd never suspect her of entertaining flirtations from another man, she'd certainly prefer to spare him the gossip. "What kind of information?"

"I'm new to town and looking for a job," the man said. "Something outdoors if I can get it. I'm good with plants, and I like hard work."

Jillian didn't doubt that, judging by the muscles that filled out the man's worn flannel shirt. "I don't know for sure, but you might try asking at Belmont Mansion. The owner, Matthew Belmont, has trouble keeping yard help. He's a grouch, but he pays on time." She didn't add that half of Matthew's problem with help was a tendency to hire sketchy people. One of his previous employees had even tried to kill her once.

The man smiled warmly at Jillian. "Thanks. Thanks a lot." He held out his hand. "Rand McCall."

Jillian couldn't see any way to avoid touching the man without seeming rude. She was sure the handshake would transform into a passionate hand clasp by the time the rumor mill was done with it. She took his hand. "Jillian Green."

To her relief, he shook her hand briefly and let it go. "Thank you kindly, Miss Green."

Jillian chose a bear claw from the pan and dropped it into a white bag before handing it over. "You're welcome. Good luck with Mr. Belmont."

He headed toward the door, fishing the bear claw out of the bag as he walked. Jillian watched him until he was out of the shop, then turned to the next customer. The woman's avid expression told her that she—and probably everyone else—had seen Jillian watching the stranger. With a sigh, Jillian hoped Hunter was as impervious to gossip as usual.

4

Despite the rainy, chilly weather, Monday night's pastry class was full. Savannah was demonstrating her technique for making the best butter rolls in town, which involved building layers of pastry dough and cold butter.

Since she wouldn't take over her part until the rolls were in the oven, Jillian took advantage of the class's attention on Savannah to drift over to the seat near the door where Louisa sat perched near the end of the chair with her tote bag in her lap. Jillian quietly moved another chair close to Louisa and sat down. "Are you okay?"

The program director looked at her sharply. "Of course."

"Forgive me, but you don't seem like it. Even the kids are noticing. I know we don't know each other very well, but I'd like to help if I can."

Louisa pressed her lips together, and Jillian braced for the woman to tell her to mind her own business. Then Louisa sighed and opened her mouth. Jillian held her breath, sure that she was finally going to find out what was making the program director so jumpy.

Bang!

Both Jillian and Louisa jumped and twisted around to look toward the back of the room where a red-faced boy chased a rolling pin across the floor. Giggles broke out around the room, and a few more teens joined in pursuit of the tool, which was living up to its name by rolling under the back counters.

Jillian stood and took a step toward the cluster of kids dropping to their knees to go after the pin. Savannah spoke up, asking everyone to return to their seats. "I have extra rolling pins. We can get the runaway after class."

Jillian backed up and sat back down, then turned to speak to Louisa, only to discover the rolling pin wasn't the only runaway. The chair beside her was empty. The program director had left during the commotion. Jillian considered going out to see if she could catch Louisa before she hopped in her car, but Savannah called out her name. It was time for her to take over the class.

Jillian's portion of the lesson went smoothly again as she talked about flavored butters and how they transformed fresh-from-the-oven dinner rolls into something truly special. She'd worried that her topic was a little dull, but the teens seemed to love the idea of coming up with their own flavor combinations from the ingredients available. Sweet butters edged out savory in popularity, and soon every student was wrapping up a tube of custom-flavored butter in waxed paper.

"You'll need to chill the butter as soon as you get home," Jillian said, raising her voice to speak over the crinkle of waxed paper. "And put it out to soften about an hour before serving."

By the time they were done packing the butter, the smell of fresh-baked butter rolls had every stomach in the room growling. Jillian appreciated Savannah sharing one of the beautiful, fluffy rolls she'd made. She resisted the urge to bolt it down, though the first bite almost melted on her tongue. "Thank you. This is wonderful."

"I'm glad to help. The growling was making me feel guilty," Savannah said with a grin as she began loading up the box of supplies.

When they hauled the boxes outside, Sidney and Celia trotted along behind Jillian, badgering her about the program director. Jillian tried to put them off with vague answers, but the teens were not easily dissuaded.

"Come on," Celia said. "You had to notice how weird Ms. Byrne was acting. When Kyle dropped that rolling pin, I thought Ms. Byrne was going to go through the roof."

"I thought *I* was going to go through the roof," Jillian said as she reached the bakery van and hauled open the door. "Being startled by something like that isn't weird."

"I know my heart was pounding," Savannah added.

"I'm telling you," Celia said, "something's not normal with her."

Sidney shook her head. "Not normal at all."

"But it's still her business, girls," Savannah said as she slipped between the two teens to put her box in the open door of the van.

It was clear the girls had more to say, but Celia's dad pulled into the lot at that moment and laid on his horn, obviously not wanting a repeat of his wait from the previous week.

"That's our ride," Celia said, as if anyone could have missed her father's arrival. "But something is going on with Ms. Byrne."

"Definitely." Sidney trotted after Celia.

Jillian leaned against the van and watched them go. As Anthony left with the girls, she said to Savannah, "I hate to agree with them, but Louisa is still jumpy. I honestly think she's been afraid to leave by herself, and I think she was about to tell me why before the rolling pin incident."

"If she was afraid to leave, where is she?"

"Maybe she was more afraid of talking to me."

Savannah gave her a wink. "It's been known to happen." She gestured around the parking lot. "At any rate, she's gone. I guess her nerves weren't as bad as you thought."

Jillian swept her gaze over the lot. Yes, Louisa was gone. But somehow Jillian wasn't at all sure that was a good thing.

Though work at the bakery kept Jillian's hands occupied for the following days, her mind remained busy with thoughts of Louisa. She was like a little kid with a loose tooth. Something was up with Louisa Byrne. It might not make sense for her to care—she barely knew the woman, after all—but something about the memory of Louisa's pale face wouldn't go away.

By Wednesday evening, Jillian had to admit to herself that she was getting a little obsessive about it, so she waited impatiently in the kitchen for Bertie to get home from class to find out if Louisa still seemed jumpy.

"I have no idea how she is," Bertie said, filling a teakettle at the kitchen sink. "She never showed. I had the fun job of keeping those youngsters on task as they set up, which was no easy undertaking." She set the kettle on the burner.

"That's odd," Jillian said. She walked to a cabinet and got down a box of chamomile tea knowing that, as Bertie's favorite evening beverage, it was probably what she'd be going for next.

"Not so much," Bertie said. "I've always thought keeping teenagers on task is like herding cats."

Jillian shook her head. "I meant it's odd that Louisa didn't come to help."

Bertie retrieved two mugs from the cupboard. "I certainly don't mind Louisa skipping the class. We don't really need her after setup, but I do wish she had let me know ahead of time. Lenora and I would have arrived a little earlier."

"Maybe something unexpected came up."

Bertie fished tea bags out of the box and dropped one into each mug. "I suppose."

"Do you know anything about Louisa's ex?" Jillian asked. "She's been acting so oddly, and I heard he'd been in trouble."

Bertie grunted. "You could say that. Being in federal prison is the very definition of trouble. I believe Louisa moved to Moss

Off to a Bad Tart 41

Hollow for a fresh start, and she has a right to that."

"I agree." Jillian leaned against the counter. "But what if something isn't letting her have that? Shouldn't we help?"

"If she needs help, she knows how to ask."

"Some people aren't good at asking for help. You should relate to that."

Bertie shot Jillian a stern glance as she filled the mugs with hot water, but she didn't spill a drop. "I don't know what you're talking about. But if you're so worried, you should call her."

"I don't have her number." Jillian winced, aware at how weak that sounded.

Bertie pulled her cell phone from her cardigan pocket and held it out to Jillian. "I do. Call her. Ask her if she's being bothered by Grange Oatley."

"Grange Oatley?" Jillian echoed.

"Her ex. She went back to her maiden name after he was found guilty."

"How do you know so much? I didn't think you knew Louisa any better than I do."

Bertie lifted her shoulders lightly in a shrug. "I don't. Annalise told me."

Never underestimate the value of the Moss Hollow gossip network. Bertie shook the phone at her, so Jillian took it and scrolled through the contacts until she found Louisa. She called before she could chicken out, trying to make a sketchy plan for the conversation in her head.

As it turned out, she didn't need it. The phone call rolled to voice mail. "Hi Louisa, this is Jillian Green. I wanted to check on you since you didn't make it to the cooking program tonight. Bertie said it went well. Talk to you later."

She handed the phone back to Bertie.

"Now when she calls back, I'll grill her for you," Bertie said picking up her mug of tea. "Until then, if you'll excuse me, I'm heading to my room."

Jillian watched her grandmother go, worry still gnawing at her.

By midmorning on Thursday, Jillian was feeling as jumpy as a cat in a room full of rocking chairs, and her distraction was affecting her work. She stared into a bowl, trying to remember if she'd put in all three cups of flour. *Does that pile of white look like three cups?*

"Why are you staring into that mixing bowl like it's a crystal ball?" her grandmother asked.

"I lost track of how many cups of flour I put in."

Bertie glanced into the bowl. "Three."

"Good, thanks." Jillian set the measuring cup on the table. "When I get a break, I'd like to drive over to the parks department office. Louisa never called back, and I'm concerned."

Bertie crossed her arms over her chest and gazed at Jillian for a moment. Then she sighed and flapped a hand at her. "Go now. I'll take over here. Maybe you'll be able to concentrate when you get back."

Jillian gave her grandmother a peck on the cheek. "Thanks. I'm sure I will." She swept the hairnet from her head and hung up her apron, then walked out of the kitchen into the front of the bakery. Normally Jillian parked in the back so she wouldn't take up any of the spaces that customers would need, but it was trash day, and as she'd hoped to slip away to the parks department office, she hadn't wanted to risk being blocked in by the garbage truck.

She knew she was risking Bertie's wrath by parking in the front, but she'd felt it would be worth it for the quick exit.

Stopping next to Maggie, Jillian poured herself a cup of coffee to take with her, then dodged around the counter to head for the front door, snapping the lid on the cup as she walked.

Her distraction over the lid nearly made her run into the man coming through the bakery door. She looked up to see Rand McCall grinning down at her. "Fancy meeting you here," he drawled.

"I'm on my way out," Jillian said. "How did things go with Matthew Belmont?"

The man's grin brightened even more. "Great. I got the job. He's a tough old bird, but I like him. And the mansion grounds are beautiful. I owe you for the lead. Maybe I could buy you a thank-you coffee sometime?"

Jillian held up her cup. "No need. I own the source. But congratulations on the job." She ducked around him before he could say anything else and slipped out the door. She suspected she was eventually going to have to explain to him that she already had a boyfriend, but such conversations were always awkward, and she was happy to put it off for another time.

The rainy days had finally passed, but they'd left a chill in their wake. Jillian shivered as she headed for her Prius, wishing she'd grabbed a sweater. She cranked up the heater in the car and headed down Main Street toward the office of the parks department, which was near the edge of town, not far from one of the larger parks where Jillian could see a dad pushing his young son on a swing. Both were bundled up against the chill, and Jillian was a little envious of their warm jackets.

She hopped out of the Prius and walked briskly to the glass double doors leading into the building. A gray-haired woman with glasses sat at a reception desk in the cramped foyer, which led to a long hallway lined with doors. She held up one finger as she explained to someone on the phone that the parks department didn't provide soccer shoes or pads for players. "We do give each child a shirt, courtesy of Food for Less, but you will need to provide other gear," the woman explained in a kind and patient tone.

Judging by the expression on her face, the person on the other end of the phone wasn't thrilled with the shirt. The woman behind the counter apologized, which seemed to placate the caller, and soon hung up. She glanced up at Jillian. "May I help you?"

"I need to speak to Louisa Byrne," Jillian said in the most pleasant tone she could muster.

"Oh." The woman's face fell. "She's not in today. Perhaps someone else could help you?"

"Probably," Jillian said. "May I speak with someone who works with her?"

Relief was clear on the receptionist's face as she stood and gestured toward the hallway. "Of course. Come right this way. I think a lot of folks are in a meeting right now, but someone should be in the program office."

Jillian followed along, examining the walls as they passed. Framed photos of kids playing various sports or on playground equipment lined the walls. The older woman opened a door and waved Jillian in. "Perfect. Bree Weston is here. She can help you." She pointed to a young woman with a head of brown curls sitting at a desk in one of about ten otherwise unoccupied cubicles separated by upholstered dividers. "She assists Louisa with several of our community programs."

"Thank you," Jillian said. She walked into the room and heard the receptionist close the door behind her. As she approached the desk where the young woman was staring intently at a computer, Jillian cleared her throat, drawing Bree's brown-eyed gaze toward her. "Can I help you?" the woman asked in a slightly breathy voice.

"I'm Jillian Green," she said with a friendly smile. "I've been helping with the teen cooking classes Louisa Byrne organized. I came in to chat with her, but I heard she wasn't in today. Is she ill?"

"I don't know," Bree said. "It's so strange. Louisa never misses work, and now this is her second day out. I even went by her house this morning, but no one answered when I knocked."

"So you're close friends?" Jillian asked.

Bree's cheeks pinked. "Not so much, but she lives near me. She's not from around here, and I hated to think of her being sick with no one to take care of her, so I went to check on her."

"That's nice of you," Jillian said.

Bree beamed at the praise. "It was no big deal."

"Has Louisa seemed like she was coming down with something?" Jillian asked. "I noticed she acted a little oddly at the last cooking class I led. She was a bit jumpy."

"She has been edgy lately," Bree said, her voice taking on a conspiratorial tone. "I don't know what was bothering her. She isn't one to complain."

"A nice trait." *But not particularly helpful.*

Bree's eager expression suggested she was just settling into gossiping with Jillian, but her mouth snapped shut as the door opened. Her face darkened. Jillian swiveled to see who had put such a damper on the cheerful young woman.

A man in his forties with a dark tan and the slightly soft look of an aging athlete walked toward them. He gazed curiously at Jillian. "Are you being helped?"

Jillian thought that was an odd question since she was obviously standing there talking to Bree. *Does he not think his coworker is competent?* She smiled at him. "I actually came to chat with Louisa, but I hear she's been out the last couple days."

He nodded, a single brisk bob of the head. "Yes. Louisa went to Macon help her sister, who is having a baby. She said she would be staying there until after Thanksgiving."

From the corner of her eye, Jillian saw Bree sit up sharply. "I didn't know that," Bree said. "Why didn't you tell us?"

"I didn't know you'd be interested."

"When did you find out?" Bree asked.

"Monday night," he said. "She called me to explain why she wouldn't be in."

"Did she sound odd or strained when you talked to her?" Jillian asked.

His expression was guarded. "Not particularly. I suppose she seemed worried about her sister. We didn't chat at length. She delivered her message and ended the call."

"Thank you for letting me know, Mr. . . ." She held out her hand and let her voice trail off, waiting to see if the man would provide his name.

He hesitated only a moment, then shook her hand. "Hinkley. Patrick Hinkley. I'll be taking over Louisa's duties until her return."

"That's good to know, in case we need help with the teen cooking program," Jillian said.

"Of course," he said without enthusiasm.

Jillian thanked them both again for their time and headed back to her car. She had an answer, but she didn't exactly feel satisfied. When she got back to the bakery, Jillian noticed that Bertie seemed tired despite having slept in. She'd been doing so much, between the bakery and the baking classes. *Sometimes it's easy to forget that despite being a force of nature, Bertie isn't a young woman.*

"Why don't you take off early?" Jillian suggested after going over the orders. "There's nothing here that Lenora and I can't handle."

Bertie gazed at her suspiciously. "Are you trying to coddle me, young lady?"

Jillian maintained an innocent expression. "I wouldn't dream of it. I just thought you might like some time off."

Her grandmother finally smiled. "I have been hoping for a spare minute to get my hair done. Cornelia was positively rude about it on Sunday."

"Don't you worry," Lenora said. "Sisters like to tease. Your hair isn't that bad."

"That bad?" Bertie reached up to touch her blonde curls through the hairnet. "I'm calling the Clip & Curl for an appointment right now."

"You tell Jasmine that I said to fit you in," Lenora said.

Jasmine didn't need much arm twisting to find a spot for Bertie, and Jillian's grandmother soon left, her gait almost springy.

Jillian and Lenora tackled the order list together and worked until near closing time. "I can take my car and drop off the bread orders," Lenora said. A number of the area restaurants only used bread from the bakery, but Bertie had driven the van to the salon, so it wasn't available for deliveries.

"Do you have enough room in your car for all that bread?" Jillian asked.

Lenora laughed. "I could take half the bakery in my car." Lenora's vehicle would be considered vintage, but not in the same way as Savannah's Riviera. Lenora's car was big, ugly, and splotched with rust, but, as she said, "I can rely on it."

Shortly after Lenora left, Maggie popped into the kitchen. "I've closed up and cleaned up, so I'm out of here."

"Did Celia come in today?" Jillian asked, glancing toward the office where they kept the schedule.

"She wasn't on for today," Maggie said. "She had some school thing."

Jillian bid Maggie good night and continued cleaning up the kitchen area in preparation for a fresh start in the morning. She found she liked the quiet in the old building. It was peaceful.

Her phone rang as she was humming while she sanitized the

stainless steel counters. She pulled the phone from her pocket, expecting it to be Bertie or Cornelia asking her to pick something up on her way home. Instead, she recognized the phone number from the call she'd made on Bertie's phone.

"Louisa?"

The voice on the other end of the phone sounded as breathless as Bree Weston, but far more tense. "Jillian. Leave me alone. Please leave me alone."

The call cut off abruptly at the end of the last word, leaving Jillian staring at the phone, completely confused.

Jillian made a concerted effort not to think about Louisa Byrne, but she slept poorly Thursday night, her dreams filled with searching for some unnamed item of great importance. She felt positively bleary the next morning, but she was determined to continue her effort to be a good granddaughter. Over a bagel breakfast, she told Bertie not to rush in. "I can get the orders going."

Bertie glanced up from her coffee mug. "Are you sure?"

"Of course." Jillian smiled at her grandmother. "I have Lenora if I need help."

"That's true." Bertie gazed at her for a long moment, her expression pensive. Finally, she said, "Actually I do need to get some things done around here, if you don't mind. I could come in by lunchtime."

Jillian was surprised that her grandmother was willing to miss that much time from the bakery. "Sounds good."

Bertie looked over at Cornelia, who was slathering strawberry cream cheese on her own bagel. "What are you doing this morning?"

"Virgil Hayes is coming to rake leaves." At Jillian's incredulous expression, she said, "We have some. Not a lot, but some."

"That is not what surprised me. Virgil said he'd never work for you again after the business with the remodel of the tobacco barn."

Cornelia waved off Jillian's comment. "People say things. I don't pay them much mind."

Considering Cornelia had said some pretty wacky things in her time, Jillian figured most of the people she knew felt much the same. She was still a little surprised about Virgil. He'd ranted for weeks about the "crazy women at Belle Haven." Virgil was another of Lenora's many cousins and a decent worker, though he never stayed on one job too long.

She noticed Cornelia was staring into her mug. "Did your tea bag tear again?" Jillian asked.

"I started buying loose tea," Cornelia said. "I dump it in the mug and add hot water. It's easier to read."

Jillian shuddered. "And easier to end up drinking wet leaves."

"I keep seeing fish," Cornelia said. "It's like they're swimming around and around in every cup." She looked up at Jillian as Bertie snorted. "Be careful of fish."

"I'll do my best." Jillian hopped up. "And with that, I'd better be on my way." She pecked each woman on the cheek and dashed out.

Later that morning, Jillian was wheeling a rack of fresh bread into the customer area when she noticed Bree Weston standing in the short line at the counter. Jillian saw that the previously vibrant young woman had dark shadows under each eye, making them appear almost bruised. She had apparently had a rough night too. "Good morning, Ms. Weston," Jillian said with a smile.

"Call me Bree," the young woman said. "You know, I'm glad to see you. Do you have a minute? After I get some cookies for the office, I'd like to talk to you about Louisa." She dropped her voice as she said the program director's name.

"Sure." Jillian ducked back into the kitchen to tell Lenora. "Do you mind if I take a few minutes to chat with a customer? I'll be right back."

"Take your time," Lenora said with a wave.

Jillian got cups of coffee for herself and Bree, then walked to the small table farthest from the rest, assuming the young woman would like a little privacy. They exchanged pleasantries when Bree sat down, then the young woman knit her fingers together nervously without speaking for a few moments.

"You wanted to talk about Louisa?" Jillian prompted quietly.

Bree bobbed her head. "I'm worried. It's not like Louisa to up and leave, no matter what Patrick said. Louisa is dedicated. Honestly, she works harder than anyone, and she's so good at this job. I wish I could be as organized and focused. Anyway, I've texted her a bunch of times, and she hasn't answered. That's not the way Louisa acts."

Jillian hesitated, wondering if she should tell Bree about the call she'd gotten from Louisa. "Maybe things are really rough at her sister's house," Jillian suggested gently. "Or maybe she forgot her cell phone at home."

"If she did, I couldn't find it."

Jillian widened her eyes. "How thoroughly did you check?"

"I sound like a creep, don't I? But I'm so worried. Louisa is super private, but she always answers messages. And when I checked out her house, the door wasn't even locked. Who goes on a trip and doesn't lock their doors?"

Jillian felt a definite pang of concern from that. As friendly and safe as Moss Hollow was, that didn't sound normal. The more she heard, the more Louisa's call last night unnerved her. "Maybe she left it unlocked so a neighbor could feed her cat."

Bree shifted nervously. "I know this sounds awful, but since the door was unlocked, I went in. I didn't see a cat. No dishes or pet food. She has a fish tank, though." She glanced down at her laced fingers. "I did check in her closet." She raised her gaze to Jillian. "I know, I'm so out of bounds, but her closet had several suitcases. Who goes on a trip and doesn't take a suitcase?"

Jillian thought of Louisa's story about the cat scratches. *Was that something Louisa made up to explain a wound she didn't want to talk about?* "Maybe she took one and left the rest. You don't know how many suitcases she owns."

"That's true. But the kitchen was messy. Well, messy for Louisa. I don't think she would leave things like that."

"Maybe her sister's need was sudden and severe," Jillian said, though she could hear the doubt in her own voice.

"I wish she had talked to someone other than Patrick," Bree said. "Not that I have anything against Patrick, but he clearly didn't have sense enough to ask questions."

Finally, the guilt over keeping quiet became too much for Jillian. "She actually has talked to someone else. She called me last night. She asked me to leave her alone. I assumed someone at your office must have talked to her about my visit."

Bree frowned. "It wasn't me. Did she sound all right?"

"She sounded tense, but if her sister is having complications, that might be the source of the tension. And as a private person, she may resent all this poking around in her life."

"Maybe." Bree picked at the tape that held the box of cookies closed, and Jillian realized this was a person who would never be able to hide her emotions. She displayed her upset in every breath and fidget. Bree took a deep breath and spoke in a rush. "I wonder if Louisa's disappearance might be related to her husband."

"Her husband?"

"Yeah, the bank robber." Bree placed her hands flat on the tabletop and leaned forward. "What if he's out of prison and he grabbed her?"

Bank robber? "But she's making phone calls," Jillian said. "And instead of asking for help, she asked to be left alone."

Bree lifted one shoulder. "Maybe she's covering for him. People do crazy things for love."

"I think we need to be careful about letting imagination eclipse facts," Jillian said, then almost winced at how much that sounded like something her grandmother would say. "So far we know of two calls from Louisa. She could have asked Patrick for help, or me. Maybe we need to leave her alone."

Bree offered a weak laugh. "You're probably right. And I'm going to have some explaining to do when Louisa comes back and finds out I was poking around in her house."

"She seems like a person who would appreciate your concern." Jillian hoped that was true, because she felt more and more that Bree was probably right. Something was going on, and it wasn't good.

Bree appeared at least slightly relieved when she left. Unfortunately, although she was glad she'd helped the young woman, Jillian felt more ill at ease now. The conversation had certainly left her desperate to do something, and she'd asked Bree for Louisa's address before she went back to work. Now all Jillian needed was a chance to head over there, but that would have to wait. She definitely couldn't leave Lenora to fill the rest of the orders on her own.

Jillian had started toward the kitchen when she heard the bell over the front door jingle, and a deep voice called her name. She faced Hunter, pleased to see a twinkle in his bright-blue eyes and a warm smile on his face at the sight of her. "Good morning. You here for cookies?" The bakery often supplied Greyson & Sons Funeral Home with treats for post-funeral receptions. "I'll even throw in a few of the chocolate scotchies we made using Savannah's recipe. They're amazing."

"Those do sound good, though the main attraction here isn't the cookies. Not for me anyway."

Jillian felt her cheeks warm at the compliment and wondered if she'd ever reach the point where she could get a kind word from Hunter without blushing. He'd certainly handed out plenty of them since they'd begun dating. Jillian hadn't dated all that many men in her life, but she was still certain that Hunter's attentiveness was rare. Plus, he was surprisingly accepting when Jillian's natural curiosity got her into complicated situations.

"I'm feeling impulsive." Hunter ran a hand through his dark hair, which was highlighted with a distinguished touch of gray. "How would you like to have dinner with me tonight?"

"That sounds wonderful. If you don't mind, I'll need to go home first if you don't want a flour-speckled companion."

"We can eat somewhere casual," Hunter said. "It's not exactly impulsive if you go home and get all dolled up."

Jillian gestured toward Hunter's immaculate silver-gray suit. As a funeral director and local coroner, Hunter was always perfectly turned out. "That hardly seems fair. Your work clothes don't much match mine."

"No worries. I have a spare pair of jeans and a sweater in my office. I keep them there so I can change if I have time to go work on the house." Hunter was slowly restoring an old rural home as a pet project.

"You win. I certainly don't want to discourage impulsiveness."

"That's my girl." Hunter leaned over and gave her a peck on the cheek, proving that he really was in an impulsive mood. Jillian heard several murmurs from the customers who were probably enjoying the show. The handsome mortician was a favorite subject of the Moss Hollow gossip mill.

Remembering her earlier plan, Jillian winced. "I will have to make one quick detour."

Hunter raised his eyebrows in question.

"A woman I know is missing," Jillian explained. "Well, sort of. Anyway, her house was left open, and I want to check and see that everything is all right inside."

"Missing sort of?"

"She has called, but it's still weird. I'll tell you all about it this evening. But I do want to run by her house."

"By or into?" he asked with a knowing smile.

"Into, probably."

"Wouldn't that be breaking and entering?"

"I'm not sure. Since the house is unlocked, it might be trespassing. But it's for a good cause. Honestly, I'm worried about the woman, and I need to do this."

"I'm not sure a local mortician should be involved in illegal activities."

Jillian cringed, realizing what she was asking of him. "Of course you shouldn't. I'm sorry. I shouldn't have asked. Don't worry about it. I'll try to get away from here for a little while at lunchtime to check out the house."

Hunter shook his head. "No you won't. I don't want you throwing yourself into this mess alone. If you think this woman could be in danger, we can stop on the way to dinner."

Jillian thanked him profusely, but after he left the bakery, she realized she now had a new thing to fret about. Was she dragging Hunter along on a very bad idea?

About an hour later, Jillian stood mixing up a batch of pumpkin muffins when she heard the back door to the bakery open. She smiled, thinking her grandmother hadn't been able to wait until lunchtime after all. To her surprise, it wasn't her grandmother who passed into the main kitchen area. It was Cornelia.

When she caught sight of worry on her great-aunt's face, Jillian asked, "Is something wrong?" She immediately pictured Bertie in a hospital bed. *I should have known something was wrong with Bertie's health when she agreed to take time off so easily.*

"Yes," Cornelia said in an artificially deep and solemn tone. "You know I've been seeing dire portents in my tea leaves."

Jillian blinked. "Your tea leaves?"

"I know you and Bertie scoffed at them, but I got confirmation this morning when I was out in the garden with Raymond."

"You know Bertie doesn't like it when you call the cat Raymond."

Cornelia's blue eyes flashed angrily. "My sister doesn't like any of my glimpses into the spirit realm. Her mind is too narrow to see the obvious. My Raymond is still watching out for me through Possum."

Jillian repressed a sigh. She knew it gave Cornelia comfort to think her late husband was still close by. And it didn't really hurt anything, she supposed. "So what was the confirmation?"

"Raymond caught a luna moth."

"Oh." Jillian winced. Luna moths were so pretty. She hated thinking they lost one to Possum's hunting habits. "I'm sorry to hear that."

Cornelia's face lit up. "So you see it."

"See what?"

"A luna moth." Cornelia stressed each syllable as if Jillian were being unusually dull-witted. "Luna moths symbolize protection. And if we're seeing a protection symbol, obviously there is something to be protected from."

"Obviously."

"And we know the danger is related to fish."

When Cornelia was like this, it was best to humor her. "Hunter has asked me out for supper. I could insist we not go to Crazy Fish Bar & Grille."

Cornelia's eyes widened. "That could be it. Maybe there is going to be an incident at Crazy Fish. I should call Laura Lee."

Jillian started to suggest the deputy wouldn't be able to act on the basis of Cornelia's otherworldly warnings, but then she decided that Laura Lee could handle this herself. "That's probably a good idea."

"And you promise not to go to Crazy Fish tonight?"

"Cross my heart," Jillian said, doing so.

"Good." The obvious relief on Cornelia's face made Jillian feel slightly guilty. As loopy as her great-aunt could be, she knew it was all from love.

Cornelia marched back out of the kitchen.

Lenora walked across the room. "You're not going to Crazy Fish tonight, are you?"

"I said I wasn't."

"I know, but I also know you don't take Cornelia's notions seriously."

Jillian raised her eyebrows. "And you do?"

"No, of course not. But it doesn't hurt to be careful."

Jillian returned to her muffin batter, wondering if everyone she knew was a little bit loopy. She made a concentrated effort to focus on the list of orders and drive out the questions and worries swirling in her head. She enjoyed the scent of autumn baking that filled the back of the bakery from the spiced batter as well as another order of pumpkin pies.

Since she was planning to go out for supper, she lunched in the kitchen on a freshly baked muffin and a cup of coffee as she skimmed the rest of the orders for the day. Bertie came in, and Jillian asked her if she'd heard about the luna moth incident.

Bertie rolled her eyes. "I did. You know, you made your great-aunt deliriously happy by agreeing to avoid Crazy Fish tonight."

"I hope Hunter is all right with it," Jillian said. "He loves eating there."

Bertie smirked. "Hunter is going to be all right with anything that makes you happy. He's wild about you. If he'd do the obvious thing and propose, you and Savannah could have a double wedding."

Jillian stared at her grandmother in alarm. "You won't say something like that in front of him, will you? I would literally die of embarrassment. Honestly, I think my heart would stop. If Hunter and I ever decide to take that kind of step, I'm sure it's far, far in the future."

"Sure it is. I'm not going to say a word to him. But you'd best be prepared. If you don't mess it up, that day is coming."

Jillian's panic subsided into irritation. Why did Bertie always assume it would be Jillian who messed up a romance? "It takes two have a relationship."

"But only one to mess it up."

Jillian started to argue, but then she remembered her bitter experience in California. Her fiancé's embezzling had been entirely his doing, and it had definitely put an end to their relationship. Of course, he'd never been the man that Hunter was.

"I'll be careful," she said finally, then popped the last bite of muffin in her mouth and went on to the next item on the order list.

Work in the kitchen hummed along for the next few hours.

Jillian intended to stay until closing, but Bertie shooed her out early to run home and change. Jillian shook her head. "Hunter told me not to get too dressed up. He wants this to be spontaneous."

"Then choose a spontaneous outfit," Bertie insisted. "But he definitely doesn't need to see you in floured-up clothes and hairnet-mashed hair."

Jillian normally kept a change of clothes at the bakery, but she hadn't replaced it after the last time she'd relied on it, so she gave in and ran home for a shower and a fresh outfit. She managed to avoid any further dire portents from Cornelia and was back at the bakery in time to meet Hunter. If he suspected she'd cheated on their spontaneity plans, he didn't mention it.

As they'd agreed, they drove to Louisa's house first and parked on the street. They walked quietly around the yard. The grass was slightly overgrown, but not weedy. Though the house had no flower beds and few shrubs, it was clearly well tended.

Hunter pointed toward the driveway. "No car, and I can see there's no garage. I assume she drives, so that supports the idea that she left of her own volition."

Jillian agreed. Nothing on the outside of the house suggested any kind of problem. They walked up the driveway and around to the backyard. A small potting shed sat near the rear fence, and its door was partially open. Jillian walked over and poked her head in. Its shelves were empty, and a lawn mower took up most of the floor space. "She doesn't seem to be fond of gardening."

"She might not have time," Hunter said. "Or have a particularly green thumb."

"That's possible. Anyway, I'll understand if you don't want to come in, but I really do need to check."

"I'll come with you."

The door was unlocked and led to a small mudroom with a vinyl floor, which was conspicuously bare of mud. Jillian didn't even see any of the cobwebs that they seemed to battle constantly at Belle Haven. They walked on into the kitchen.

On the kitchen counter were two coffee cups, both about half-full of liquid and swimming in mold. Jillian wrinkled her nose. She opened cupboard doors and peered inside. The contents of every cupboard were precisely arranged and impeccably neat. Jillian figured that even Bertie couldn't find fault with Louisa's sense of order.

"That's weird," Jillian said.

Hunter was opening cupboards. "Well, it suggests a neatness obsession, but I don't know about weird."

"Not the neatness, though that is a little much. I meant the contrast. Look at how neat she keeps every single cupboard, but then she leaves two cups of coffee to mold on the counter? That seems to be the opposite of what you'd expect from someone like her preparing for a trip."

"Maybe she left in such a hurry that she simply missed them," Hunter suggested. "Especially if she was worried about her sister. Even a careful housekeeper can make a mistake."

"Then why are there two cups?" Jillian asked. "Louisa lived alone. And she hardly appears to be the sort who would dirty a second mug instead of washing up."

"Someone must have been here with her," Hunter said.

"That would be my guess, and whoever it was might have some insight into what's going on."

"Assuming what's going on isn't just a woman visiting her sister."

"Yes, assuming that," Jillian admitted.

They walked into the living room and Jillian froze. A large fish tank stood near the front windows. For an instant, she thought of Cornelia's warning about fish. *Don't be silly*, she scolded herself silently, then she marched across the room to peer into the tank—and recoiled.

No fish moved around in the water. Instead, they all floated at the top of the tank, dead.

"Hunter," she said softly. "Why would someone as detail-oriented as Louisa leave her pets to die?"

Hunter scrutinized the fish. "Maybe she didn't expect to be gone as long as she has been, and she didn't have anyone she could ask to feed them."

Jillian bent to examine the fish tank stand's lower shelves and pointed. "There's a box of slow-release fish food here. It says it's good for a month. If she used this, there's no reason for the fish to be dead."

Hunter had continued to stare at the tank. He laid a hand on Jillian's shoulder. "I don't think the fish starved."

Jillian straightened up. "What makes you say that?"

Hunter pointed into the tank. Nestled in a bed of multicolored gravel, half-hidden by plastic plants, was a handgun.

"Oh," Jillian said. "That doesn't belong there."

"No, I don't think it does."

At that moment, a loud banging at the front door made both Jillian and Hunter jump. A familiar voice shouted through the door. "Nathan County Sheriff's Department! Open this door at once!"

Jillian and Hunter glanced at each other. "Gooder," she whispered.

Hunter smirked. "Busted."

Jillian trudged to the front door. It wasn't that she didn't think that law enforcement should be involved. They'd found a gun in a fish tank—of course they needed the police. But needing the police and needing to spar with Gooder Jones were two different things.

It was obvious the deputy felt the same way. He groaned loudly as soon as Jillian flung open the door. "Jillian, what a surprise," he said. "I should have known it would be you by the sudden pain I got in my neck as I came up the walk."

"You're so very amusing. I avoided a dressing-down from your grandmother the other day, but I guess today I won't be so lucky." Jillian crossed her arms and sighed, remembering how relieved she'd been to be spared Ophelia Jones's razor tongue.

"Nana Fee rarely says anything that doesn't need to be said."

Hunter stepped forward. "Hello, deputy."

Gooder rolled his eyes. "I can't believe you let her rope you into this."

Behind Gooder, a portly woman in a housecoat and curlers poked Gooder. "What are you doing?" she demanded. "These two are clearly burglars. Arrest them!"

"Please, Ms. Ward, stay calm," Gooder said to her. "I know both of these people. They aren't burglars."

The woman narrowed her eyes at Jillian and Hunter. "They're inside Louisa's house when she's not here. That makes them no-goodniks."

Jillian blinked. *No-goodniks? Where did this woman come from?*

"I'm sure Ms. Byrne appreciates having such a concerned neighbor," Gooder said. "And thank you for calling us. You go on home, and I'll handle this from here. I'll come by for your official statement before I leave."

For a moment, Jillian thought the woman would protest, but she finally turned around with a loud huff and stalked off, grumbling that Gooder was probably going to get his head blown clean off.

Gooder crossed his arms over his chest. "So tell me, Jillian, am I going to get my head 'blown clean off'?"

Jillian crossed her own arms. "No, but it's interesting you should ask. We found something you need to see."

Hunter stepped up and spoke in his smooth, calming voice. "We were actually about to call you. We have made a rather disquieting discovery."

"More disquieting than breaking and entering?" Gooder asked as they backed up to let him through the door.

"Considerably," Hunter said before Jillian could jump in and explain that they may have entered, but they hadn't broken anything.

"I think Louisa Byrne is missing and not simply away," Jillian said. They walked the few feet to the fish tank and she pointed. "And I think that's a big fat clue."

"That does look like a clue," Gooder said. "Do you suppose it's what killed the fish?"

"How would it do that, Gooder?" Jillian asked. "They don't appear to have been shot."

"It could be possible, I suppose," Hunter said diplomatically. "If some gunpowder leaked out of the bullets or it brought in some sort of bacteria. Ms. Byrne has been missing for a few days, which I suppose is long enough for fish to have been affected by whatever the gun introduced into their environment."

Gooder stared at the gun through the fish tank glass. "This

Louisa Byrne—how do you know her? And what makes you think she's missing?"

Jillian launched into what she knew about Louisa and her disappearance, talking fast since she could see Gooder wasn't in a patient mood. As she talked, Gooder continued to stare into the tank, and Jillian suspected he was trying to come up with a way of getting the gun without sticking his hand in a murky tank full of dead fish. Finally, he gave up, shucked off his jacket, and began rolling up his sleeve. As she had finished her recounting of events anyway, Jillian paused. "You could put a plastic bag over your hand and arm to keep the muck off."

"I don't have any evidence bags that would be big enough." He shot her a glance. "Do you happen to have a plastic bag that isn't covered with trace evidence?"

"I do," Hunter said. "I carry a box of small trash bags in my glove box. They're perfectly clean. I can go get one."

"Best bring the box so I can get one out that hasn't been contaminated," Gooder said.

Hunter nodded and headed briskly out the front door.

As soon as he left, Gooder said to Jillian, "So you're basing this little breaking and entering event on a hunch and some remarks by imaginative teenagers, despite the fact that the woman has called twice since her so-called disappearance?"

"One of her coworkers is concerned as well," Jillian said defensively. "Plus, she sounded strained over the phone."

"An extremely private woman who found out you were poking around in her affairs sounded tense? How remarkable."

"You know, your attitude could use adjusting," Jillian said.

"It's been adjusted. I used to be a happy man before you moved home."

"Oh good, you two are still fighting," Hunter said as he walked in with a box of trash bags. He handed the box to Gooder, who gave

Jillian a last glare before carefully plucking out two bags with his gloved hand. He set the first aside and slipped the second one over his arm. He flipped open the lid on the fish tank topper and thrust his arm in. Immediately, he jerked it back out. "That water is hot!"

"Hot?" Jillian echoed.

"Not boiling hot, but too hot for a fish tank," Gooder said.

Jillian touched the back of her hand against the side of the tank. Sure enough, it was warm. "I think we know what killed the fish. I killed my goldfish that way when I was a little girl. I thought she might be cold so I added warm water to her bowl. It was very traumatic."

Gooder examined the tank hood. "This thing is more than a light. It's also a heater, and it's cranked way up. Why would anyone do that?"

"To kill the fish?" Jillian suggested.

"Intentional fish murder? Why is every case connected with you so weird?" Gooder thrust his arm back into the tank and retrieved the gun. He raised the barrel to his nose and sniffed, then winced. "I have no idea if it's been fired lately. It smells like rotten fish tank." He pulled the bag off his arm, turning it inside out over the gun and using it as an impromptu evidence bag. "I don't have any evidence bags on me that would fit this. Somehow I wasn't expecting to be bagging up handguns today."

"In Moss Hollow, I imagine it's difficult to know what to expect," Hunter said mildly.

"It is." Gooder aimed a smirk toward Jillian. "Unless I know she's involved, and then I know to expect a disaster."

"It's not that I don't appreciate sparring with you, but you seem unusually grumpy," Jillian said. "Is something wrong?"

"Let's focus on the task at hand," Gooder said. "I think you should leave this whole thing alone, Jillian. For all we know, Louisa's concern for her sister had her in a panic. That could make anyone forgetful enough to leave a mess in the kitchen. And maybe she was worried the weather would get cold, so she turned up the heater for the fish."

"Which still doesn't explain the gun." Jillian shook her head. "I've been worried about family many times, but never enough to confuse a handgun with a box of fish food."

Gooder shrugged slightly. "That is odd. Listen, if I were doing my job, I'd arrest both of you for breaking and entering."

"The door was unlocked," Jillian insisted, then stopped talking when Hunter gently squeezed her hand.

"That would be reasonable," Hunter said mildly. "Shall I call my lawyer now? And I could put in a call to Judge Riley. I handled the funeral of his favorite aunt last month, and he said to call if I ever needed anything."

Gooder groaned. "I'm not arresting you. I know you didn't break in to steal anything."

"We didn't break in," Jillian repeated. "It was unlocked."

Gooder ignored her and focused on Hunter. "You really should think carefully before taking part in one of Jillian's harebrained investigations."

Hunter smiled, but Jillian could see the tension in his jaw. "Thank you for the advice. Here's some for you. I suggest you check into Ms. Byrne's disappearance. She doesn't sound like a woman who stores guns in her fish tank, leaves cups of coffee to mold in her kitchen, cooks her pet fish, or leaves her doors unlocked."

"If it'll keep you two off my back, I'll track down this woman's whereabouts and make certain she is there of her own free will," Gooder said. "Now, please, no more trespassing."

Since Jillian appreciated his downgrading the accusation from breaking and entering to trespassing, she smiled sweetly at him. "I wasn't planning any more."

"Good."

Over dinner at a tiny new restaurant in Painter's Ridge that promised farm-to-table dining, Jillian widened her eyes at the menu. Apparently farm-to-table dining was pricey.

"What are you having?" she asked Hunter.

"A steak," he said. "The filet here is amazing."

"It better be. And it ought to come with a side order of gold coins."

Hunter grinned at her. "For a second there, I thought I heard your grandmother."

"I think I did too," Jillian said sheepishly. "The prices surprised me. When you told me not to dress up, I was expecting something a lot less haute cuisine and a bit more Cheap, Cheap Chicken."

"It's simple food, not fancy," Hunter said. "When you buy from family-owned farms, the ingredients may be expensive, but they're fresh. And I'm okay with the prices because they help local farmers stay afloat."

"Still." Jillian glanced around the room. "I'm a little under-dressed for the crowd." She was grateful that Bertie had made her go home and change. Her dark-teal sweater and charcoal slacks couldn't compare with the dresses on some of the women in the room, but at least she wasn't horrifically embarrassed. Hunter managed to make his own sweater and jeans seem classy. Of course, he could make ripped denim and flannel seem dressy by how he carried himself.

"You look lovely," he said, and she felt her cheeks warm at the compliment, however undeserved. "Do you mind if I ask you about something?"

Jillian set the menu down, giving him her full attention.

"Shoot." She expected he'd have some question or caution related to her concerns about Louisa Byrne.

Hunter laid his own menu down. "I am not particularly worried. I trust you. But I am curious about the handsome stranger I've been hearing about. A man hanging out at the bakery."

Jillian rolled her eyes. "He's been in twice, which is hardly hanging around."

"I wasn't being accusatory. I've been in Moss Hollow long enough to know how the gossip mill works. But I am curious."

"Fair enough." She related the two encounters with Rand McCall. "I was only helping the man find a job."

He reached out and took her hand. "That was kind of you. Assuming he and Matthew Belmont don't end up killing each other."

"Actually, Rand said he likes the old man."

"So you're on a first-name basis with this handsome stranger?" Hunter raised an eyebrow. At Jillian's annoyed expression, he laughed. "No, honestly, I'm not concerned. I know better than to think you'd be flirting with anyone else."

Jillian frowned as he returned to his menu, then tried to figure out what was triggering her annoyance. Was it because Hunter had brought up the topic in the first place? Or was it his easy confidence that he had nothing to worry about? After all, Rand was quite good-looking. Did Hunter think a man like that wouldn't be interested in her? The more questions that popped into her head, the more annoyed she became.

Stop being silly, she scolded herself as she pretended to scan her own menu. It's a good thing that this hadn't become a fight. No matter how much she tried to quell it, though, a thread of annoyance kept pushing its way in, making the rest of the evening awkward. Jillian was glad when they finally headed back to the bakery so she could pick up her car.

Before she could hop out of Hunter's Lexus, he caught her hand. "Jillian? Is everything all right?"

Jillian could feel the tension in the smile she pasted on her face. "Of course. Thanks for dinner, and for your help with Gooder."

The expression on his face was equal parts concern and puzzlement. She felt guilty and wished she knew what to say to make things normal again, but she still wasn't quite sure what had made her so upset with him. She leaned over and pecked his cheek. "I should run. I have an early day tomorrow."

"Of course." He let go of her hand, and she hopped out of the car, feeling like she was fleeing a fight that had never really happened. She puzzled out her emotions on the trip home. She wasn't sure what was bothering her, but she was pretty sure she wasn't being completely fair to Hunter. "That's the thing about emotions," she said aloud. "They don't care about fair."

She rolled down the window and let the chilly night air cool her face, which still felt flushed from the stress of the evening. To keep from running questions about her relationship through her mind like a hamster on a wheel, she forced her thoughts back to Louisa's house. She didn't have any more answers there.

With the chill in the air, the loud buzzing and chirping of night insects, which could reach an almost painful volume in the summer, had softened. When she got out of the Prius at Belle Haven, Jillian paused to enjoy the night. She walked around the house, soaking up the mildly spooky feeling of being out wandering the yard after dark.

The cool breeze tossed her long red hair and made her glad for the sweater she wore. The moon was nearly full. Jillian glanced up at it, picking out the face. Gazing at the moon brought back a sudden memory of her grandfather, Jack. He'd had great appreciation for the night sky, and he especially loved folktales associated with the constellations and the moon.

She remembered one night he'd pointed up and asked, "Do you see the face in the shadows on the full moon, Jilly?"

"Yes," she'd said, squinting to bring it in focus.

"Some people see a bunny in those same shadows. Can you see him?"

Jillian had stared for a long time before she'd seen the bunny. She'd squealed when she picked him out. "I see him!"

"Good. You know there's a lesson in that, my girl. Two people can look at the exact same thing and see something different. If you want the whole picture, you need to see with your eyes and with theirs."

Jillian smiled at the memory. She had been thoroughly confused by the idea of trying to see with any eyes other than her own, but now she realized it was good advice. Sometimes it helped to step back and examine things from a different perspective, letting the shapes form something totally different in her head.

The front door of the house opened, spilling light across to the toes of Jillian's shoes. "Are you going to come in?" Bertie asked. "Or are you courting a cold? I was on my way out to get you."

Jillian crossed the short distance and stepped into the house. "Out to get me where? You knew I was with Hunter."

"We got a phone call," Cornelia said as she approached. "We heard you were at the sheriff's department under arrest for breaking and entering. Bertie was going to go bail you out."

Jillian groaned, wondering how the Moss Hollow rumor mill had gotten that idea. "That's ridiculous. I was certainly not arrested. I was having dinner with Hunter."

"Was that before or after you burgled Louisa Byrne's house?" Bertie asked.

"Where are you two getting this?"

"Juliet Ward told Marie Torenson," Cornelia said. "Juliet lives next door to Louisa Byrne, and Marie lives on the other side of Juliet."

Jillian crossed her arms over her chest. "I met the Ward woman. She was with Gooder."

"At Louisa Byrne's house?" Bertie asked. "Where you should not have been?"

Jillian ignored that comment. "So this Ward woman told her neighbor. How did it get to you?"

Cornelia began counting off contacts on her fingers. "Marie called Patsy, the one who works down at the post office. Patsy called Jasmine, which is like broadcasting it over the television. Jasmine called Lenora, and Lenora called us. It took us a few minutes to raid all of Bertie's hiding places for cash so we could come bail you out."

"Hunter and I were never under arrest," Jillian said. "And I'm not sure bail works that way, though I appreciate that you were going to try."

Bertie and Cornelia both raised their eyebrows. "Hunter went with you on a burglary?"

"It wasn't a burglary. Or breaking and entering," Jillian insisted. "One of Louisa's coworkers said the house was unlocked. I was worried. Hunter and I stopped there to see if the house was still unlocked. Juliet Ward apparently saw us and called the sheriff's department. Gooder was, as always, a delight."

"Gooder Jones was where he was supposed to be because you were not," Bertie said sharply.

"Bertie, a woman could be in danger. I had to do something."

Her grandmother sighed, and Jillian saw the fight go out of her. "I know. You have a good heart, but you made me worry. It's possible that the story was distorted as it was passed around."

"Significantly," Jillian said.

"Either way, I'm glad you weren't arrested. And if Hunter was with you, I'm sure you were fine."

Jillian felt a flair of annoyance. "I can take care of myself, you know."

Her grandmother patted her arm. "Sure you can. I'm heading to bed. I'm glad you're home. Good night."

Jillian watched her grandmother shuffle off and felt the tiniest pang of guilt. She hadn't done anything wrong—well, not very wrong—and she'd still exhausted Bertie with worry.

She was pulled out of her remorseful musings when Cornelia plucked at her arm. "So tell me about Louisa Byrne's house. What did you find?"

Jillian told her and then winced at the clear delight on Cornelia's face.

"A fish tank with a gun." Cornelia made a tsking sound. "I told you the tea leaves were warning about danger and fish."

"You told me not to eat fish for dinner," Jillian said.

Cornelia sniffed. "A small misinterpretation. The important thing is that I was right. I hope you'll pay more attention to my readings now."

"I'll do my best." Jillian gave her great-aunt a hug and headed up to her room. She was more than ready for bed herself.

She was brushing her teeth in her small bathroom when she heard her phone buzzing on the nightstand. She hurried in and snatched it up, managing to catch the call before it went to voice mail. "Hello?"

"Leave things alone!" Louisa Byrne gasped into the phone. "Please!"

"Louisa, what's wrong? Please, tell me what's going on."

The call ended, leaving Jillian begging with no one to hear.

8

As the time to open the front door of the bakery approached the following morning, Maggie called into the kitchen, "Can someone come out here and open the door? I need to be behind the counter when they come in."

Jillian hung the order clipboard on the hook. "Sure." It wasn't unusual for there to be one or two people waiting outside for the bakery to open. On Mondays, it sometimes rose to half a dozen as people lined up, desperate for coffee and pastries to get going at the beginning of the week. As soon as Jillian passed through the kitchen doorway, she saw this was not a usual Saturday.

A crowd stood outside the door, and several more people peered into the bakery through the big display window, hands cupped around their eyes. "Are we giving away free bear claws today and no one told me?" Jillian asked as she crossed the customer area.

"I have no idea what's going on," Maggie said.

Jillian turned the lock and opened the door. People rushed in, shoving one another and nearly running Jillian over. To her surprise, they didn't head for the counter. Instead, they clustered around her, all demanding to know if she'd heard the news.

"What news?" she asked. She saw Stewie Franks shuffle on past the fray and head for the counter, where he was certain to get his usual order so he could settle down to read the newspaper. *At least one person is still acting sane.*

"About the Byrne woman," Bess Holland said.

"You burgled her house," Gordon Sprague offered helpfully.

"I didn't burgle anything," Jillian said. "What about Louisa Byrne?"

Gordon blinked at her owlishly, clearly not really expecting that anyone would have to explain. "She's in the hospital."

"Ben Conahue ran her over," Bess added.

"He couldn't help that," a voice added. Jillian didn't notice who had spoken as the knot of people around her pressed in. "She ran right out in front of his truck."

"That's what *he* says," another voice chimed in.

"You calling Ben a liar?"

Jillian held up her hands and shouted, "Hold on! I get it. Louisa was in an accident. Why are you all here?"

All around her, people blinked in surprise.

"To get a bear claw," Gordon said.

"And talk about the accident," Bess added. "And find out what you know."

"Bear claws we have," Jillian said, her voice still raised to be heard over the chatter around her. "But I don't know anything else. What you just told me is news to me. I don't even know who Ben Conahue is."

"He's been in here before," Maggie called out from behind the counter. "He's an older guy. Kind of rumpled. He seems confused a lot." Maggie's description didn't help much since it matched at least two of the people in the bakery at the moment.

"Ben's not that old," Gordon muttered, scratching his own graying temple.

"Everyone calls him 'Old Ben,'" Maggie said.

Gordon frowned at her. "I don't."

Since Jillian had nothing useful to add, the chatter dissipated into disappointed grumbles. A few members of the crowd simply left the bakery, but the bulk of the visitors lined up in front of the counter and continued to chatter away. The citizens of Moss Hollow were nothing if not committed to their gossip.

Jillian slipped behind the counter to help Maggie deal with

the crowd. As she poured cups of coffee, she acquired most of the known details—and more than a little speculation. Late the previous night, Louisa Byrne had run out into the old road that edged Becker's Woods. Ben Conahue was heading home after playing cards with his buddies. He was tired, and everyone said Old Ben's reflexes weren't what they used to be. He'd run Louisa over. She was in the hospital, and everyone agreed that her situation didn't look good.

With all the basic details sorted out, Jillian was left with bigger questions. What was Louisa doing in the woods when she'd told a coworker that she was leaving town to stay with her sister? Could this be related to her husband? What if he'd escaped from prison and dragged Louisa off to the woods? Maybe she'd even helped him escape.

Jillian handed a tall cup of coffee to the last person in line. She was letting her imagination run away with her. What she needed was the truth, not speculation. And she had a pretty good idea where to get some facts.

With the customers all contentedly served and dishing gossip from the tables around the room, Jillian headed back into the kitchen. Bertie and Lenora both turned curious gazes toward her, and Jillian held up her hand. "I promise to tell you everything I know. In just a minute."

She walked to a quiet corner near the tall cooler and pulled out her cell phone. Laura Lee answered immediately and whispered, "Hold on."

Jillian waited, assuming Laura Lee was getting out of earshot of Gooder, who often didn't approve of her conversations with Jillian.

"I assume this is about Louisa Byrne," Laura Lee finally said, her voice soft but no longer whispering.

"Well, yes and no. How is she?"

"Not good."

"How terrible." Jillian felt a twist of guilt that she was fairly certain was undeserved. She didn't know how she could have helped Louisa, but she had tried. But she had a sinking feeling that she could have tried harder. "Do you know her room number at the hospital?"

"She's in intensive care. They won't let you in." But Laura Lee told her the room number anyway.

"Thanks," Jillian said. "I'm actually calling about Louisa's husband. I'd like to know exactly what he did to land himself in prison. And I'd like to know whether he is still in prison."

"You think he has something to do with Louisa? Jillian, she was run over by a truck. We know that. Ben Conahue doesn't dispute it."

"Sure, but what put her in the middle of Becker's Woods when she said she was leaving town to help a sick sister? And what drove her to run into the road late at night? This is more than an accident."

"I should be able to dig up the answers about her husband easily enough, but I don't know what you think it'll prove."

"I don't know either. I'm trying to put a puzzle together in the dark, and I'm missing pieces." Jillian glanced over at Bertie and Lenora, glad to see her grandmother wasn't giving her the stink eye yet. "Oh, and can you tell me anything about the handgun Hunter and I found in Louisa's fish tank?"

Laura Lee groaned. "Are you trying to get me fired or something? You know Gooder would blow a gasket if he knew I was talking to you."

"Gooder blows so many gaskets, it's a wonder *he's* not in the hospital," Jillian said.

"True. The gun's serial number was filed off. The lab restored part of it, but matching a partial number on a handgun in the South is a pretty big job. There are a lot of registered handguns in Georgia."

what that deputy said. I saw you break into Louisa's home. I know all about corrupt policemen. I watch television."

"Too much, from the sound of it," one of the nurses seated at the station muttered.

Juliet spun to glare at the small group of scrubs-clad hospital employees, clearly unsure which one had made the remark. The angry head nurse pointed from Juliet to Jillian. "This is no place for a squabble. If you two cannot get along, I'll have to ask you to leave. Or I'll call security, and they won't ask so nicely."

"Fine," Juliet spat, the word sharp as a dagger. "But I insist this woman not be allowed anywhere near my dear friend Louisa."

"Your dear friend?" Jillian asked, actually curious. "I hadn't heard Louisa was close to anyone."

Juliet tilted her chin loftily. "I always make a point of becoming friends with my neighbors when I move to a new place. A strong community watches after one another."

"Please, ladies," the nurse said, her voice more weary than angry now. "Can you take this somewhere else? Neither of you is going in to see Ms. Byrne at this time."

"But she's my friend," Juliet said with a whine.

The nurse was unmoved. "And she needs rest and quiet."

"Fine. I'll be back." Juliet stomped away.

Jillian glanced toward the room marked with the number Laura Lee had given her. Since she clearly wasn't going to get in, she should leave. But for some reason, she felt a great reluctance to abandon Louisa here. Instead, she walked to the small waiting area, which was empty and gave her a clear view of the nurses' station.

Jillian sat down and thought about the weirdness of Louisa Byrne being hit by a truck when she was supposed to be with her sister. For a moment, Jillian wondered if Louisa even had a sister. It was about this time that she noticed the nurses' station was empty. No one peered at charts or pecked away on a computer keyboard. No one talked softly.

She glanced toward Louisa's room and saw movement. But none of the nurses had gone in, she was sure of it. Was Louisa up? That seemed unlikely if she was in intensive care. Worry edged Jillian's nerves.

Stepping out of the waiting area, Jillian looked up and down the halls. There was no one likely to yell at her, so she walked swiftly and quietly to Louisa's room. She quickly solved the mystery of who was moving around inside it. The person standing beside the injured woman's bed was neither a nurse nor a doctor. It was Patrick Hinkley, the man from the parks department, the one who'd reported Louisa's plan to visit her sister. Patrick stood close beside Louisa's bed, carefully adjusting her pillow.

"I thought the hospital wasn't allowing visitors in here," Jillian said quietly from the doorway.

He turned sharply. "They aren't. They let me in because I lied and told them I was Louisa's fiancé." Jillian widened her eyes in surprise at his revelation, and he smiled sadly. "It's really more wishful thinking than a lie." He gently lifted a strand of hair away from Louisa's pale face. "I wish I had spoken up and told her how I felt. You wouldn't believe how many times I've rehearsed telling her. I was a coward." His voice thickened as he added, "I hope I have another chance."

"You could tell her now," Jillian suggested. "They say unconscious people hear more than you'd expect."

His expression brightened with hope. "You think so?"

"It's what I've heard."

Jillian examined Louisa. She had a bruise that ran down the side of her face and contrasted sharply with her skin's pale pallor. A monitor kept track of the injured woman's vital signs, but none of its numbers meant much to Jillian. She noticed a clear bag of liquid hung from a pole trailing a tube that ran to Louisa's arm. Jillian hoped whatever was in it was helping.

Her gaze traveled back to Louisa's face just as the woman's eyes flew open. Jillian gasped. "She's awake."

"Louisa!" Patrick said. "I'm here."

Louisa's gaze fell on him, full of alarm and confusion. She stared around wildly, spotted Jillian, and lifted a hand toward her. Jillian stepped closer and took it. "You need to go get a nurse or a doctor," Jillian said to Patrick. "They'll want to know she's awake."

"Right." Patrick backed out of the room.

Jillian held Louisa's hand gently, not wanting to cause the woman any further pain. "You're in a hospital. You were hit by a truck, but the hospital is taking good care of you. You're going to be fine." Jillian wasn't sure if the last part was the truth, but maybe saying it would make it so.

Louisa's mouth opened, and she struggled to say something. She tossed her head restlessly.

"Stay calm," Jillian said. "A doctor will be here in a moment. Are you in pain?"

Louisa's eyes locked on hers and her mouth moved more. Jillian leaned closer, in case the woman was speaking, but she didn't hear anything.

"Try to relax," Jillian coaxed.

Suddenly, Louisa's eyes widened dramatically, her gaze on something behind Jillian. She began to wheeze and claw at her own throat. The monitor beeped some sort of alarm. A nurse pushed Jillian out of the way to reach Louisa, and Jillian continued in reverse, making space for the medical professionals pouring into the room.

With her eyes still locked on the bed, Jillian backed up until she bumped into someone behind her who settled a hand on her shoulder to steady her. She turned to see Patrick and Juliet, both fixated on the bed with eyes full of horror.

A man in a long white coat stepped into the room. Without making eye contact, he commanded, "Go. Let us work."

"Of course," Jillian said. She stepped into the hallway and the other two trailed her. The monitor alarm continued to sound in the quiet ward.

"What did you do to her?" Juliet demanded.

"She didn't do anything," Patrick said. "Louisa had some kind of attack. You saw that part same as I did."

"But who knows what she did before that, when she was alone in the room?" Juliet was clearly unconvinced.

Jillian didn't bother answering. She couldn't tear her eyes away from Louisa's door, which was now closed. Each shrill beep of the monitor, still audible despite the barrier, seemed to cut through her. Then she heard the worst sound of all. The monitor's shrill alarm ended abruptly. And all they heard was silence. Dead silence.

Jillian wanted to stand outside the closed door until someone came out with a report, but the nurses shooed them away. The intensive care unit didn't allow loitering, and now that the alarm had been silenced, she formed a mental picture of the doctor and nurses working to revive Louisa. Jillian didn't think it was likely that she'd be able to sit quietly in the tiny waiting area with Patrick and Juliet. In fact, judging from the hostile glares coming from Juliet now, Jillian half-expected the woman to launch into more noisy accusations. Instead, the portly woman simply scowled at Jillian and Patrick, and then stomped out of the intensive care unit.

Patrick drifted to the waiting area as though only partially seeing what was going on around him. Jillian followed him. "When you talk to a doctor, would you call and let me know how she is?"

"Of course." Patrick dutifully took Jillian's number, then whispered, "What you said about unconscious people hearing what you say: Do you think that's what brought on that last seizure, or whatever it was? Maybe she didn't like what I said. Do you think it's my fault?"

"I'm sure it's not," Jillian said. "She was hit by a truck. That's what happened."

He nodded, but Jillian doubted he was convinced. She patted his arm a bit awkwardly and left.

Jillian made it as far as her car before she started shaking. Had she witnessed Louisa's last conscious moments? The injured woman had clearly tried to tell her something, but what? She thought angrily of the accusations Juliet Ward had made, suggesting Jillian had done something wrong when alone with Louisa. After all, Patrick had clearly been alone with the injured woman for some time—why no accusations for him?

Jillian gripped the steering wheel, but she knew she was in no shape to drive yet. She fumbled for her cell phone and called Hunter. "Do you have a minute to talk?" she asked softly as soon as he answered.

"Of course, Jillian. What's wrong? You don't sound good."

"I'm not, but I'll be okay. Could I come to you?"

"Of course. I'm at the funeral home, doing some paperwork. Do you want to come here? Or should I meet you somewhere?"

Jillian thought about asking him to come to the hospital, but that seemed self-indulgent. He was working, and she was an adult. She needed to pull herself together. "I'll come to you." She called The Chocolate Shoppe and told Bertie she was running by the funeral home to talk to Hunter before coming back to the bakery. As she expected, Bertie was completely in favor of that. Anytime Jillian was with Hunter, Bertie was happy.

By the time she was done with her calls, her hands were steady and Jillian felt capable of driving.

Located at the edge of town, Greyson & Sons Funeral Home occupied a sprawling beige Victorian with a big wraparound porch. The many additions gave the place a homey and welcoming feel, while the classic lines and elegant decor reassured mourners that their loved one was properly honored and respected.

To Jillian's surprise, it was Hunter who met her as she walked into the foyer. Usually she was led to Hunter's office by his assistant, Oliver Kent, a rather high-strung young man who peered out at the world through round glasses and was often confused by what he saw. "Where's Oliver?" Jillian asked.

"Visiting his mother," Hunter said. "It's her birthday weekend.

Which reminds me that I ought to find a gift for my own mother's birthday. Is Santa Fe too warm for a cashmere scarf?"

"I think it gets cold there in the winter. That sounds like a present befitting New Mexico's premier pottery artist." Jillian hadn't yet met Bernadette Greyson, who had relocated to the Southwest to chase her dream of becoming a professional potter after Hunter had moved to Moss Hollow. Hunter's father had passed away when he was young, leaving Bernadette to raise Hunter alone. Grateful for all the love and care she'd given him, Hunter had fully supported her move—even if it did mean he rarely saw her.

"I'm sure if you approve, it'll be perfect." Hunter took Jillian's hand as they walked down the hall. Jillian was struck, as always, by the peaceful atmosphere of the old building, enhanced by the walls painted a warm cream and trimmed with deep crown molding.

Hunter squeezed her fingers gently. "So what's troubling you? Are you all right?"

"Not so much." Jillian leaned into Hunter's shoulder as they walked, liking the feeling of calm strength that always radiated from him. "I went to the hospital to see Louisa Byrne. You heard about her accident?"

"Oliver told me when he called in this morning to see if I needed him to rush back. I told him I'd be assuming the best and that he wouldn't be needed. How he is keeping up with Moss Hollow events from Atlanta, I do not know." He peered at her closely. "I take it the hospital was rough."

"You may have assumed too much when you told Oliver to stay in Atlanta." She launched into a recap of the morning's events. They reached his office as she was still relating the over-the-top reaction of Louisa's neighbor.

Hunter waved her in ahead of him. "The neighbor seems like a person who likes being the center of attention."

"I did get that vibe." Jillian sank down in one of the comfortable chairs facing the desk.

"I'm sure you have more to tell me, but can I get you a cup of coffee?"

"That would be lovely. Should I come with you?" She started to rise.

"No, sit. I'll get the coffee. You gather yourself." He left the office door open as he headed to the kitchen near the back of the building.

Once she was alone in the large office, she could finally feel herself relax a little. Hunter's office echoed the same feeling of understated class as the rest of the building. The furniture was mostly antiques, beautifully cared for. But despite that, questions whirled in Jillian's head. Had Louisa actually seen someone behind Jillian who alarmed her? Was it Patrick? He'd sounded sincere about having feelings for Louisa, but Jillian knew from experience that she wasn't always the best judge of when someone was telling the truth. She'd been fooled before. "I need to learn more about him."

"More about whom?" Hunter asked as he walked through the door.

Jillian took the mug of coffee from him. "Patrick Hinkley. He worked with Louisa and is the one who reported on her call about visiting her sister. He was at the hospital, in Louisa's room. Apparently, he told the staff he was her fiancé so he could get in. When I walked in, he was messing with her pillow."

"And that struck you as suspicious?" Hunter sat in the chair beside her rather than walking around the desk to his usual seat.

"Not at the time." Jillian took a sip of the dark, rich coffee. "But now, everything is striking me as suspicious."

"Why are you digging into this so hard? The woman no longer needs you to find her. And you barely know her. Why is it bothering you so much?"

"I don't know. I still feel like something important is unfinished, and I'm looking at it, but I'm not seeing it." At Hunter's confused expression, she explained how her grandfather had helped her see the shadows of the moon in a new way. "I'm certain the shadows of Louisa's life make an important picture, but I can't see it yet. And I can't let it go. And on top of that, I'll be leading the class on Monday. The kids know Louisa"—she blanched—"or knew Louisa, if it comes to that, and they're going to have questions. What do I say to them?"

"How about the simple truth? You don't know."

"I don't." Jillian took another sip of her coffee to give herself a moment to think. Then she told Hunter about her last moments in Louisa's room. "I saw what may have been her last conscious moments. And I'm certain she was scared of something."

"I imagine she was afraid of dying."

"Maybe. I don't know."

Hunter reached out and took Jillian's hand again. "I don't know what you should do, but every time you get tangled up in something, you endanger yourself. That worries me. I would feel a lot better if you let this go."

Jillian didn't voice the thought in her head: *And I wish you'd support me even when it makes you uncomfortable.*

As that thought lingered in her mind, it was interrupted when her phone rang. Without a moment's hesitation, she accepted the call. It was Patrick. Louisa had died shortly after Jillian left the hospital.

The Sunday Sweetie Pies meeting buzzed with the news of Louisa's death.

Jillian raised her hand and waved to get the attention of the whole group. "Does anyone know anything about the place where Louisa was hit by the car?"

"I know the spot," Laura Lee said, frowning slightly at the pumpkin cupcake on the plate in front of her. "I saw some of the photos of the accident site. There's nothing particularly unique about it, except that someone told me the old oak tree across the road is some kind of landmark."

"The Lovers' Oak?" Savannah asked, her voice nearly a yelp. "Really? She was found near the Lovers' Oak?"

"Why don't I know what that is?" Jillian asked.

"Because you already had a boyfriend in high school," Savannah said.

"Huh?"

"The Lovers' Oak is an old legend," Bertie said. "A particularly foolish old legend."

"You would say that," her sister said sharply. "You have no romance in your soul. The legend is that if a young woman who is truly in love carves the name of the man she adores into the tree under a full moon, he'll dream of her."

Jillian raised an eyebrow at Savannah. "And you knew that legend?"

Savannah's cheeks pinked. "Well, there may or may not be a certain name that was carved into the tree on the night of a full moon right after you broke up with him."

"I didn't break up with him," Jillian argued. "Nadine stole him." She shook her head, not wanting to revisit her days as a suspect in Nadine Belmont's murder. "Okay, we're wandering off topic. I'm less interested in the oak tree by the road than the woods itself. If she ran out of the forest, she had to be running from somewhere. What's out there? Is there anything a person might venture in to see?"

"Deer." Maudie reached for a cupcake. "The woods have a lot of deer, and there's at least one old hunting cabin out there, assuming it hasn't fallen down in the last few years. There might be more."

"Since when do you know what's out in the woods?" Wanda Jean asked, peering at her friend suspiciously from over the rim of her coffee cup.

"Hugh went through a hunting phase until he figured out you couldn't watch sports in the middle of the woods. But some of his buddies still hunt out there, and I remember them mentioning the cabin, so I figure it's still standing."

"I know some folks who've camped out in it," Laura Lee said. "Though I'd rather sleep in a tent than a cabin some animal might already be calling home."

"I'd rather sleep in a bed," Jillian said, but she wondered if Louisa might have been at the cabin for some reason, possibly even against her will. "How close is the cabin to where Louisa was hit?"

"Not close," Laura Lee said. "And if I were hiking from the cabin to the road, I'd come out at a different spot."

"But what if you didn't know the woods and someone was chasing you?"

Laura Lee smirked. "That's a lot of supposition. There's not really anything interesting around there. We're thinking maybe someone dropped Louisa off near where she was hit, though we don't know why. She may have started into the woods, and when she heard the truck, she rushed back out at exactly the wrong time."

"Which still leaves the question of why someone would drop Louisa off near the woods," Jillian said.

"Maybe she got mad at whoever was driving," Annalise suggested. "I remember once when Byron and I were dating, I got so mad at him I made him stop the car and let me out. It was way out in the boonies, and poor Byron followed along behind me in the car, begging me to get back in." She giggled at the memory, apparently now a sweet one.

"At least he didn't drive off and leave you," Savannah said.

"That's one of the reasons I knew he was a keeper." Annalise took a bite of cupcake.

Jillian put an elbow on the table and cradled her forehead in her hand. "I don't understand. If someone took Louisa to the woods, who did it and why?"

"I've tried to find answers in the tear-out cards," Cornelia said, which elicited matching groans from Bertie and Jillian. Cornelia was convinced her collection of magazine subscription cards, mostly gathered from the Clip & Curl, could provide a glimpse into the future. Cornelia gave Jillian and Bertie each a scowl before continuing. "I can't get any reasonable response. It's frustrating."

"I'm sure it is," Savannah said consolingly, and Jillian gave her friend a sideways glance. As much as Jillian would prefer people didn't encourage Cornelia's more eccentric fancies, she knew Savannah found them charming.

Lenora cleared her throat. "If you ask me—which you haven't, but you should—I'd focus on that fellow you said was in Louisa's hospital room. How come he's lying and lurking around in the ICU? And how come he's the only one who heard this crazy sister story?"

"We're trying to track down the sister," Laura Lee said. "But her contact information wasn't on anything in Louisa's house or work desk." Laura Lee picked up her coffee cup and added, "Not that you heard any of that from me." She took a nonchalant sip.

The rest of the Sweetie Pies launched into a lively discussion of the merits of Patrick as a suspect, though no one could be certain what he might be suspected of doing. Annalise thought he could have been about to smother Louisa with a pillow. Maudie offered the suggestion that maybe he had injected something into Louisa's IV and the attack happened to coincide with Jillian's visit. Cornelia said they shouldn't ignore the possibility of a curse.

As the wild theories bounced around the room, Jillian leaned closer to Laura Lee. "Anything you can tell me about Louisa's ex-husband?"

"First, he's still her husband," Laura Lee said softly. "There are no records of divorce proceedings. Apparently, Louisa went back to using her maiden name without ever divorcing the guy. He's still in the federal prison in Atlanta."

"Do you know what he did exactly?"

"He was convicted of embezzling from the building company where he worked in Athens. I called one of the lead detectives on the case. He said Grange Oatley never revealed what he'd done with the money. He keeps insisting that he's innocent."

"How much money are we talking about?" Jillian asked.

"Around $300,000." Laura Lee took another sip of coffee while Jillian processed the enormity of that amount. "The detective said he can't imagine how Oatley ever thought he would get away with stealing so much, but Oatley's not talking. The detective also said he considered it lucky that that missing money didn't trigger some kind of treasure hunt. People always get hurt when something like that happens."

"Maybe that's what happened to Louisa," Jillian said. "She was taken by someone who wants the money."

"There's zero reason to think she has it. She lives modestly, well within her income level. Her closet held no extravagant clothing, and she didn't own any jewelry to speak of. Her car was old. If she was hiding a few hundred thousand dollars, she certainly wasn't enjoying it."

"So where is the money?"

Laura Lee raised her coffee cup in a kind of salute. "That is the $300,000 question. If you figure it out, be sure to let me know."

Jillian didn't answer. She was more interested in another question. *Did that $300,000 get Louisa killed?*

On Monday morning, Jillian offered to go in early again so that she could justify sneaking away later on her break. Again she was surprised at Bertie's easy agreement. Jillian could remember when her grandmother was nervous to leave Jillian alone in the bakery for fear of a catastrophic brownie fire, but that was well behind her. Jillian had conquered nearly all the Chocolate Shoppe recipes and had even come up with a few inventive creations of her own. "Guess I grew up to be a baker after all," she said aloud in the quiet bakery kitchen.

The morning stayed busy with plenty of orders to fill. Jillian doubted she could have stayed on top of things without Lenora's help, but she was still glad to give Bertie some time to herself. To her surprise, she'd only been at the bakery about two hours before her grandmother bustled in.

Jillian stood at the long stainless steel table, cutting out a batch of autumn sugar cookies. "I thought you were going to stay home until closer to lunchtime."

Bertie rolled her eyes. "Cornelia was being unbearable. She was carrying Possum around looking for the spot in the house with the 'thinnest veil.'"

Jillian's forehead wrinkled. "We haven't had a veil in the house since we hosted a wedding on the lawn."

"That's what I said. So my sister informed me that she was talking about the veil between worlds. That's when I decided I'd had enough rest for the morning. So, where are we on the order list?"

Lenora snatched up the clipboard with the orders on it and

walked Bertie through what they'd accomplished. Jillian let the bakery details wash over her as she pressed leaf-shaped cutters into the soft dough. She carefully transferred the cookies to a baking sheet and sprinkled them with sugar that had been tinted shades of gold, red, and dark green. She carried the pan to the oven, and Bertie followed her over.

"Once the cookies come out, you're free to go."

Jillian gave Bertie what she hoped was an innocent expression. "What makes you think I want to go somewhere?"

"Past experience. I know you're not done with this Louisa Byrne thing."

Jillian set the timer for the cookies. "I would like to go over to the parks department office. For one thing, I want to make sure the teen program is still on."

"Why wouldn't it be? It was on while Louisa was away."

Jillian snapped the magnetic timer against the oven. She gave Bertie a sheepish smile. "Fine. I want to quiz Patrick Hinkley under the guise of checking on the status of the program. You heard the supposition at the Sweetie Pies meeting. Patrick is definitely suspicious."

"You know the Sweetie Pies like a good conspiracy theory, right?" Bertie asked. "I wouldn't necessarily take that as guidance."

"Yes, but I don't know where else to start, and I feel like I have to do something. I practically saw the poor woman die."

Bertie poked her arm lightly. "Which doesn't make you responsible for her."

"No, but it makes it hard for me to let it go."

"Fine. Get out of here." Bertie flapped a hand at her. "I'll watch the cookies. The sooner you do it, the sooner you'll be more settled."

"Have I told you lately that you're a fantastic grandmother?" Jillian asked as she leaned over and kissed Bertie's cheek. Her off to a Bad Tart   97

grandmother fussed, but Jillian could tell by her pink cheeks that she was pleased.

Jillian pulled the apron over her head. As she hung it on one of the hooks on the wall, she peeked through the doorway to the front of the bakery and considered grabbing a cup of coffee to take with her. She really liked the pumpkin spice flavor they'd added for the season. Her gaze scanned the crowd in line at the counter, and she spotted Rand McCall. *That settles it. I don't need coffee enough to rev up the gossip engine over Rand and his muscles again.*

To avoid bumping into him, she went back through the kitchen and headed for the rear exit, pulling off the hideous pink hairnet as she reached the garbage can closest to the door. She tossed the hairnet into the trash and headed out. The slightly pungent scent in the back alley made Jillian think it was past time for them to wash out the small Dumpster the bakery shared with the hardware store next door. Her grandmother insisted they do that periodically to avoid the smell that burned Jillian's nose. *Do normal people ever wash out Dumpsters?*

She hustled to her Prius. The air was too warm for a jacket, but Jillian suspected it would be cooler without the buildings around her shielding her from the fall breeze. She rolled the windows down a little as she made the short trek to the parks department building.

The receptionist had added a row of tiny pumpkins to the edge of her desk. She smiled brightly at Jillian, then her smile dimmed. "I remember you," she said. "You're Louisa's friend. I'm so sorry for your loss."

"I expect you knew Louisa better than I did, working with her every day. I didn't know her very long."

"She was in and out a good bit," the receptionist said. "And she often seemed preoccupied. But she was always so nice. Anyway, can I help you?"

"I actually came in today to see Patrick Hinkley," Jillian said. "I'm part of the teen cooking program, and I need to talk with him about the rest of it."

"He's here. Go on back. You know the way."

Jillian thanked her and walked down the hall of doorways. She walked into the room of cubicles, which were mostly filled today, and approached Bree Weston's desk. "Is Patrick Hinkley here?"

Bree bobbed her head. "He has his own office. Next to Louisa's." She pointed to a plain door at the other end of the room. "If you feel the urge to take him with you when you leave, have at it."

Jillian was surprised by the edge on the remark. "Is he giving you trouble?"

Bree looked around at her coworkers, all of whom seemed particularly intent on their computers. "He's taking over Louisa's duties with a lot of zeal." Her mouth tightened into a disapproving line. "It's unseemly. We haven't even heard anything about Louisa's funeral plans yet, and he's already taking over."

"Maybe it's his way of dealing with missing Louisa."

"We all miss Louisa," Bree said. "But only one of us is becoming a dictator."

"Maybe we could chat later?" Jillian asked. "After I talk to Patrick."

Again, Bree's gaze darted around the room. "Not here."

Jillian was still facing Patrick's office door so she saw when it opened. She quickly stepped away from Bree and crossed the room as Patrick emerged. He held himself stiffly, and he seemed surprised to see her. "Can I help you, Miss Green?"

"I came to ask about the status of the teen cooking program."

"It will continue," he said. "The program is popular, and we're getting some excellent press from it. Of course, I won't be coming by during any of the sessions. I don't cook, so I can't see what assistance I could be."

"Louisa always helped set up the room."

Patrick's expression grew horrified. "Are you talking about moving tables and setting up chairs? That was certainly . . . helpful of her."

"Louisa was a very helpful person," Jillian said.

"Yes, of course. I suppose I might be able to find someone to come out and help with setting up tables." He looked across the room as if trying to choose a minion to do something he clearly considered beneath him.

"I'm sure we'll be fine," Jillian said. "We have several teens who come early to help, and they know where everything is."

Relief was obvious on his face. "That's good."

"If you need one more hand, I could come," Bree called out. Jillian turned to see her rising to her feet behind her desk.

"That's quite industrious of you," Patrick said. "But Miss Green has said she's fine."

Jillian suspected this was Bree's attempt to arrange a meeting for them to talk. "Well, another adult to help keep the kids on task would be helpful."

Patrick's face reflected mild annoyance, but Jillian suspected it was more because he thought Jillian couldn't make up her mind rather than an attempt to keep Bree away from her. "Fine. By all means, Bree, help out with the teen program tonight." He waved a hand in a vague gesture, and Jillian thought his fingernails appeared so well-groomed that he might have had a manicure. "And any other night they might need."

Bree beamed. "I'll be happy to."

Jillian suggested Bree arrive a bit early, thinking that would give them a chance to talk before the teens showed up. The young woman agreed.

Patrick had clearly decided the whole matter was settled as he bid Jillian a firm "Good day."

Jillian echoed the sentiment, then left, casting a quick smile toward Bree as she passed her desk.

By evening, the moderate day had grown cool enough for Jillian to slip into a jacket. Because she intended to chat with Bree, Jillian pulled the bakery van into the parking lot of the community center well ahead of Savannah's arrival. She saw Bree had gotten there first and stood leaning against a blue coupe, her arms crossed over her chest.

Jillian swung the van into a parking spot nearby and hopped out. "Thanks for coming so early. I hoped we could talk for a minute before anyone else got here."

"I'm good with that." Bree laughed nervously. "Sorry for all the cloak-and-dagger, but Patrick has been such a pain. I think he's been dreaming of taking over the office ever since they hired Louisa. He was expecting to be promoted into that spot, and he was so ticked when they hired her instead."

Interesting. "Did Patrick ever show signs of being romantically interested in Louisa?"

This time Bree's laugh sounded more spontaneous. "I never thought of Patrick as being capable of being romantically interested in anyone. He seems like one of those robots on a science fiction movie. He looks human, but is he?"

"So, no sign of interest?"

Bree paused to think about the question. "I wouldn't say that exactly. He never flirted with Louisa, but he never flirted with anyone else either. I couldn't imagine that, and if I could, *ew.* Anyway, I did see him staring at Louisa a few times without her noticing. I always figured he was imagining himself in her job."

"Would you call them wistful stares?" Jillian asked.

"No, more blank and weird. Which is kind of how I'd describe Patrick in general. I've always thought he was a smidge old and creepy. But Louisa never seemed creeped out by him."

"Did she seem interested in him?" Jillian asked. "Friendly?"

"Louisa was nice to everyone, but she didn't show him any special attention. She also didn't avoid him or anything like that."

As Jillian considered another question, Savannah pulled her cherry-red car into the lot and brought the conversation to an end. Bree helped them unload the supplies, and, by the time they had everything inside, the teen helpers had arrived. Bree supervised them, joking with the teens as they worked, although Jillian noticed that Avery and Faith both seemed more subdued. That same mood was reflected in most of the participants as they arrived.

Jillian noticed that Avery even had red-rimmed eyes. "Are you all right?" she asked gently.

Avery nodded. "It's weird, coming here after Ms. Byrne is gone. We saw her at a bunch of different programs this year. She was nice." She sniffled.

"It's weird," one of the boys said. "You know old people are going to die, you know? But Ms. Byrne wasn't that old. And getting smooshed by a truck is a bad way to go."

"Michael!" several of the girls half shouted at him.

"Gross. And not true." One of the girls spun to look at Jillian, her ponytail whipping out behind her. "That's not true, right? She wasn't smooshed."

"Um, no," Jillian said. "She was knocked down and badly hurt." She really hadn't been prepared to talk about relative physical damage brought on by a truck hitting a person.

"I'm sure you all knew Ms. Byrne better than we did," Savannah said. "Though she was clearly very nice."

"She was," Celia said. "But she's been gloomy and kind of crabby during this cooking program. She snapped at one of the chefs teaching the Tuesday class. I'd never heard her do that before."

The ponytailed girl seemed a little scandalized by Celia's criticism. "You're not supposed to say mean stuff about dead people."

Michael piped up in Celia's defense. "Hey, she's telling the truth. Ms. Byrne used to be a lot more fun."

"She had good reason to be sad," Faith said. "On account of her husband being in prison and all."

"He's been in prison the whole time since she moved here," the boy argued. "Why would it make her grouchy now?"

"Sometimes it takes a while to hit people," Avery said.

"He must have been a skunk to end up in prison," Celia said.

"He was cute though," the ponytail girl said. "I saw a photo when I checked out the details online. He was good-looking for an old guy."

This received a chorus of "Ew!" from around the room.

The girl lifted her chin defiantly. "An old guy can be cute. And he probably looks even better now. Everyone knows prisoners spend all their time lifting weights. He's probably really buff."

"You watch way too much TV, Brittany," Michael quipped.

"Maybe you could use a little prison time, noodle arms," she shot back.

As the group laughed, Jillian began to feel bad about letting the teens gossip about an adult, especially since it was devolving into name-calling. Savannah clearly felt the same way, because she clapped her hands to call attention. "As interesting as that is," Savannah said, "we need to move on to baking. Tonight, we're talking about filled pastry, and we're going to make a variety of tasty fillings."

The teens quickly got on task and buffeted Savannah with

questions, switching mental direction completely when the subject changed to desserts.

Jillian began unloading bags of prebaked cannoli shells. They'd decided to focus on the filling rather than having the teenagers make the delicate pastry. As she worked, Jillian thought about the stray remark Brittany had made about muscles and prison. For some reason, her mind turned to Rand McCall. She remembered their first meeting when he talked about his desire for outdoor work. His skin tone had not reflected his apparent passion for being outdoors. Didn't men in prison tend to be pale? Could Rand be an ex-con? And could he be associated with Grange Oatley somehow?

The class went well, as they all had. Even when the teens made mistakes, they seemed to adapt quickly and not let the blunders get them down. Jillian wished she'd had more of that attitude when she'd first come back to Moss Hollow and tackled work at the bakery. It might have made those early days much less painful.

Bree left about halfway through the class, waving from the doorway and promising to stay and help take down next time. Many of the teens lingered at the end, and the group made quick work of putting away the tables and chairs. Soon, all they had left was carrying packed cartons to the bakery van.

Once they were outside, Celia and Sidney cornered Jillian, pressing her for information about Louisa. "We need a direction for our investigation," Celia said.

Jillian halted, nearly making the teens plow into her. "Stop. Right now. This situation has gotten far too serious for you to use it as an exercise for practicing your sleuthing skills. A woman is dead."

"Yeah," Celia said. "We noticed. You forget, we knew her."

"And liked her," Sidney added. "Besides, we've already learned something."

Jillian knew she shouldn't encourage them, but the words slipped out of her mouth before she could rein them in. "And what's that?"

Sidney and Celia wore matching triumphant expressions. "This creepy guy took over Louisa's Sunday evening self-defense program," Celia began.

"We don't take that one," Sidney interjected. "But I have friends who take it, and they say the guy is really serious and crabby."

Celia shot her friend a glare, and Jillian suspected she didn't feel like she needed help telling her story. "Anyway," Celia said pointedly, "last night, one of the guys in the program said he saw the man outside crying in his car."

"Someone should look into that guy," Sidney said. "Because maybe he was crying from guilt."

Jillian figured the creepy guy in question was probably Patrick Hinkley. She again told the girls that they should leave the investigation alone, but she found herself wondering about the man's behavior. Was he crying because of his secret affection for Louisa? Or did his tears have a darker explanation, as Sidney had suggested? Jillian decided that Sidney was right. Someone certainly did need to look into that guy.

On Tuesday morning, Bertie took one look at Jillian shuffling into the Belle Haven kitchen for breakfast and said, "Don't even suggest I come in late. I can tell you're going to need a keeper today."

Jillian made her way to the coffee maker. "I don't need a keeper. I'm fine."

"Sure you are."

Cornelia glanced up from her cup of tea. "Have you noticed any new theater groups in the area?"

"I don't think so," Jillian said. "The high school is probably doing a Christmas program though. Are you wanting to go to something?"

Cornelia set the cup carefully down on the table. "No, no. I have been checking my tear-out cards. I keep getting one from a drama magazine. I think it's something to consider."

Bertie rolled her eyes. "I've said it before: Your trying to find meaning in magazine subscription cards is the silliest thing I've ever heard."

Cornelia lifted her chin. "I'll have you know that reading tear-out cards is an old and respected method of connecting to the spirit realm. Ayesha over at the Clip & Curl says so. And her grandmother has the Sight."

Jillian wondered how Cornelia had gone so long without realizing Ayesha had been talking about tarot cards, but since she had no interest in seeing Cornelia mess with those, she kept the knowledge to herself. "I'll keep an eye out for actors."

Cornelia smiled at her. "Good. I knew you'd be sensible."

Bertie gave her a glare for encouraging her great-aunt, but Jillian pretended not to notice as she sat down at the breakfast table and grabbed a slice of toast. "Do we have a lot of orders today?"

"It's nearly Thanksgiving," Bertie said. "Yes, we have a lot of orders."

Bertie was never one to suffer fools gladly, but she was being unusually crabby. Jillian frowned at her. "Are you all right?"

"I'm fine," her grandmother snapped. "But my sister thinks she's a carnival fortune-teller, and my granddaughter thinks she's Nancy Drew."

Jillian knew that both of those things did annoy Bertie, but neither was anything new. "No, that's not it. Something else is bothering you. What is it?"

Cornelia reached over, snagged a slice of toast from the pile, and began buttering it. "She has her physical this afternoon."

"Oh, that's it." Jillian knew Bertie liked Dr. Taylor well enough. What bothered her were the tests and the scolding she always got about working too hard.

Bertie narrowed her eyes. "No, that's not it. A physical is a perfectly normal yearly nuisance. I'm a grown woman. I don't let things like that bother me."

"Then why are you being such a grouch?" Cornelia asked.

"I'm not being a grouch. Now if you two will excuse me, I need to get to the bakery." Bertie hopped up and stalked out of the kitchen.

Cornelia took advantage of her sister's absence to hand Possum a scrap of bacon. "It's the physical."

Jillian gazed after Bertie. "It could be a rocky morning."

It was. Between Bertie's cranky temper and Jillian's distraction over Louisa's death, the morning became a series of accidents, until Bertie finally stood in front of Jillian, steam practically billowing from her ears. "You need to go do something else," she scolded.

"Go ask some nosy questions. Go turn over some rocks. But go. Get your head clear before you come back here. We have too many orders for you to be distracted."

"But your appointment—" Jillian started.

"Is late this afternoon," Bertie said. "Just be back by then."

Jillian hated to leave her grandmother with so much work, but she caught sight of Lenora nodding vigorously and realized she was acting as a catalyst for Bertie's temper. It would be better for everyone if she gave her grandmother time to calm down, so she stopped stalling and headed out to her car.

For a moment, she sat behind the wheel and tapped her fingers. "Okay, so now where do I go?" She had to choose between two important questions: What were Patrick Hinkley's real feelings for Louisa? And was there something about Rand McCall she ought to know?

Since the second question was the newest, Jillian made her decision. She pulled out of the small parking lot behind the bakery and headed for Belmont Mansion. She spent most of the drive psyching herself up for a chat with Matthew Belmont. Remembering the cranky old man's unpleasant manner made Bertie's present mood seem positively giddy. Nevertheless, for some reason, he liked Jillian, though she'd be hard-pressed to say why. After all, both of his daughters hated her. Jillian had even been suspected in the death of one of them, and she'd gotten the other one arrested for murder. Logically, Jillian should be the person he detested most in Moss Hollow. *Which goes to prove that Moss Hollow is not a normal place.*

When she reached the estate, she was struck as always with how different it was from Belle Haven, even though they were both old plantation homes. At Belle Haven, the house and the landscaping made frequent use of curves, from the arched front windows and stained glass dome over the sweeping staircase right down to the gently curving driveway. Belmont Mansion, on the other hand, was angular almost to a fault, with square columns and little ornamentation.

Jillian pulled into the parking area near the front door and trotted up the wide steps. When she rang the bell, she tapped her foot nervously as her gaze swept the front lawn. It was flawlessly maintained. *Well, even if Rand is up to no good, at least he's doing a nice job on the lawn.*

"Jillian!"

At a familiar voice, she spun sharply and saw the smiling face of Allie Jamison. Allie was Matthew's nurse and general companion. She was also the cheeriest person Jillian had ever met. That cheerfulness had once made Jillian suspicious, but now she knew it was genuine. Allie simply saw the world as full of wonders and joy.

Allie hugged Jillian tightly. "Long time no see," she said, with a hint of scolding.

"The bakery is eternally busy," Jillian said. "I was hoping to talk to Mr. Belmont."

"Come on in. I'll see if he's available." Allie waved her into the house. "I'm sure he will be. Hold on a sec." The young woman dashed away while Jillian stood in the foyer, admiring an urn of flowers. She hadn't waited long when Allie reappeared. "He wants you to come to the office. Do you know the way, or do you want me to come with?"

"I can manage. Thanks, Allie."

Allie gave Jillian another impulsive hug. "I'll be in the kitchen. Can you pop in before you leave?"

"For a minute."

The younger woman beamed before spinning on her heel and trotting off. Jillian took a deep breath, mentally preparing for what was sure to be a challenging chat, and headed to the office of Matthew Belmont.

The office was all dark wood and leather, and Jillian could tell every piece of furniture—from the heavy desk to the leather chairs—was expensive. Matthew had made a minor fortune by literally building a garbage empire. Belmont Sanitation had been the sole garbage pickup service for most of Nathan County for years, and now the company handled recycling as well.

Matthew wasn't behind the desk, nor was he sitting on any of the comfortable leather chairs. Instead, he was bundled in blankets and sitting in a large electric wheelchair. He'd lost weight since Jillian had last seen him, and now he sported an oxygen cannula in his nose. She felt a pang of sadness and sympathy at the clear show of decline.

"What a surprise, Miss Green," the old man said. "Are you getting impatient for your inheritance?"

Jillian groaned. The fact that she was in Matthew's will had once nearly gotten her killed. It was one of the many things about the old man that made no sense to her. "I was hoping you had changed that by now."

His eyes twinkled. "Wouldn't you like to know?"

"Not particularly. I hope you live a good long while. And I hope to keep our interactions as minimal as possible during that time."

That remark set Matthew laughing, which settled into a gasping cough. Jillian looked toward the office door, wondering if she should go get Allie. "Do you need help?"

He shook his head and waved off the suggestion, so they both waited until he had finally caught his breath. "I do like you, Miss Green. You should come by more often. What brings you out here today?"

"I understand you have a new yardman."

His eyes narrowed. "Rand McCall. He said you recommended he come talk to me."

"I did. I know you have trouble keeping help, seeing as how

you're a grouch. I figured you'd probably run off several gardeners since I was here last."

Matthew chuckled. "Maybe a few. I suspect Rand is made of sterner stuff."

"And I suspect he might possibly be an ex-con."

"Of course he's an ex-con," Matthew said. "It's one of my favorite things about him. With an ex-convict, you know what you're getting. That hasn't exactly been true of some of my past employees."

"Do you know what he was in prison for?"

He shifted position in the wheelchair to sit up straighter. "Don't know. Don't care. He works hard, and that's what he's hired to do."

"Do you know where he's staying?"

"Here, in the gardener's house." Matthew harrumphed. "It's not much more than a shed, but it has electricity and a bathroom, and Rand hasn't complained."

"Does he leave the grounds much?"

"Nope. He goes into town every morning to get me some baked goods. I have a sweet tooth, as you might remember. Allie is a good cook, but she can't bake like your grandmother."

"Few can," Jillian said.

"I give the boy a day off, of course. I'm no ogre. He spends most of it reading. When I told him he could borrow books from my library, he practically cheered. Never seen a gardener so fond of books. He ought to go to college, but then, who would take care of my grounds?"

"That's a good point." From the sound of things, Rand didn't have a lot of time to have been involved with Louisa's disappearance, though she doubted Matthew could watch him that closely. "I'd better be going. I appreciate you seeing me."

"You're welcome. Next time you come, bring muffins or some of those bear claws."

"I will," Jillian promised.

Mathew motored his wheelchair over behind the desk. "You can see yourself out. Be sure to speak to Allie. That silly girl likes you even more than I do."

After saying goodbye, Jillian left the office and walked to the kitchen. The smell of coffee greeted her before she walked through the doorway. The kitchen at Belmont Mansion was smaller than the one at Belle Haven, but clearly outfitted with the best of everything. Jillian knew the cost of the appliances from their own shopping when they'd had to remodel the Belle Haven kitchen after a fire.

"Jillian, I hope you've got time for a cup of coffee," Allie said.

"A quick one. It smells wonderful."

"Mr. Belmont imports a special kind, but he doesn't mind if I drink it. He's a wonderful boss," Allie said cheerfully, making Jillian smile. She rather doubted anyone had ever said that about Matthew before.

Jillian sat on one of the high stools at the counter. "Allie, do you know the new yardman?"

"Of course," Allie said as she poured coffee in two blue mugs. "I don't know him all that well, but he's nice. He's kind of a flirt, but I figured I've been there and done that. So I've been keeping my distance."

"You know about his past?" Jillian asked as Allie passed her the mug of coffee.

"You mean prison? Yeah. At least he's up-front about it." Allie leaned forward with her elbows on the counter and her mug between her hands. "Are you still dating Hunter Greyson? He's seriously handsome."

"Mm-hm," Jillian took a sip of the rich coffee. It really was delicious. "I am, and I agree."

"I don't know if I could get used to the whole funeral home

thing." Allie winced before brightening again. "But for the right guy, I'd be willing to try."

They talked for a while about Hunter and then general Moss Hollow gossip. Finally, Jillian caught sight of the clock on the wall. "I'm sorry, but I need to run. My grandmother has a doctor's appointment."

"Okay, but we should hang out more. Send my love to your grandmother. I wish I could bake like her."

"Don't we all? Thanks for the coffee." Jillian handed Allie her empty mug and got off the stool. Allie immediately began cleaning up, which got Jillian to thinking. "You're a detail-oriented person."

Allie paused, her expression quizzical. "I have to be. I have a lot to keep up with. Mr. Belmont's meds alone require a chart."

"Imagine you were leaving on a trip. It's kind of an emergency. Would you leave a mug of coffee on the counter?"

Allie wrinkled her nose. "Ugh, no. Never. Can you imagine how gross that would be when you got home? How long does it take to rinse a mug and leave it in the sink?"

"That's what I figured." Jillian headed out, hoping she wasn't leaving Allie thinking she was crazy. The image of the moldy cups on Louisa's counter was in her mind. Two moldy cups. Not only had Louisa not cleaned up, she hadn't cleaned up after a guest. *But who?* Could it have been Patrick Hinkley? Or maybe even Rand? After all, just because Matthew thought Rand didn't leave the property much, that didn't mean he'd be aware of it if Rand left quietly. And the man was an ex-con. What if he knew Louisa's husband in prison and had heard about the missing money? He might have paid Louisa a visit—a visit she never got the chance to clean up after.

Jillian walked out of the house and headed for her car, her mind still whirling. As jumpy as Louisa was, would the woman have let a stranger into her home if she didn't know him? It seemed more likely that she would have welcomed Patrick since she knew him from work.

"I need to find out who drank that coffee," Jillian whispered to herself. Then she smiled grimly. There was one person nosy enough to likely already know the answer.

Just as Jillian laid her hand on the handle of the driver's-side door, she was startled by a deep voice. "I thought that was you." She whirled to face Rand McCall, who stood behind her holding an alarmingly sharp-looking pair of hedge trimmers.

"I came by to see Mr. Belmont," Jillian said. "He mentioned you in complimentary ways."

Rand wiped at his forehead with the back of one wrist. "Mr. Belmont is a great guy."

His remark startled a laugh out of her. "I seriously doubt that's a sentence many people in Moss Hollow have uttered. You have to admit, he can be unpleasant."

"Compared to the people I've had to deal with in the last few years, Mr. Belmont is a sweetheart." Then he took a step closer to her. "And speaking of sweethearts, there's something I've been wanting to ask you. Would you have dinner with me sometime?"

"That's very flattering, but I'm seeing someone."

Rand took another step closer, and Jillian had to resist the urge to step back. "Yeah, I heard about that," he said. "Honestly, the undertaker? You could do better."

Annoyance flared inside Jillian. "And you'd be better?"

"Than an undertaker? Yeah, I think so." Rand's confident smile suddenly slipped away. "Oh, I know what's going on. Someone told you that I did time in prison. That's behind me. I made a mistake, and it was stupid and wrong, but I paid for that."

"I'm not refusing because of your past." Jillian crossed her arms over her chest. "It's funny you'd assume I won't date you because you've been in prison, but you say I should stop dating Hunter because he's an undertaker. You don't see the double standard there?"

His grin was back, albeit now a bit sheepish. "Yeah, I guess I do. Fine, you're dating someone. He's a lucky guy."

"Which is something he's said as well." Since the topic of Rand's prison time had come up with no provocation from her, she decided to go with it. "So where were you in prison?"

He shrugged. "Florida mostly, though I got a transfer in the last few months because of overcrowding. I finished up in Atlanta, in the federal prison there. Not that it mattered much to me. A cage is a cage."

"Did you happen to know someone by the name of Grange Oatley?" Jillian asked.

He paused to think about it. "The name doesn't sound familiar. Was he in Florida?"

"No, Atlanta."

Rand shoved his free hand into the pocket of his jeans and rocked back on his heels. "That explains it. He wasn't my cellmate, so I wouldn't have known him. I only had a couple months left when I got to Georgia. I didn't spend time making friends."

Rand certainly sounded sincere, but she'd had trouble spotting lies before. And who would be better at lying than an ex-convict? Still, Jillian had no reason to call him on it. "Well, I should run. I'm needed at the bakery. It was nice to see you."

"You too. And if it doesn't work out with the undertaker, I'm still interested."

"And persistent," Jillian said.

"Faint heart never won fair lady," he said, then laughed at Jillian's surprised expression. "We watched a lot of old movies in prison. And I like to read."

"So Mr. Belmont said. You're certainly an interesting man."

His face brightened with hope. "Interesting. Now that sounds like something I can work with."

"I'd rather you didn't. Have a good day." Jillian hopped in her car and focused on what to do next. She really did need to get back to work, but there was one more stop she wanted to make. According to her car's clock, she had just enough time before Bertie would need to leave for her doctor's appointment.

Jillian headed toward Louisa's house. Considering how meddlesome Juliet Ward seemed to be, Jillian didn't imagine Louisa could have had visitors without her nosy neighbor noticing. The only question would be whether the hostile woman would talk to Jillian at all.

It turned out that Juliet's curiosity was greater than her hostility, since she grudgingly invited Jillian in. "Your house is charming," Jillian said, then felt bad for basically lying. Juliet's home was a hodgepodge of what appeared to be thrift-store finds, all used to the point of near collapse. Jillian mentally compared the mess to Louisa's impeccably neat house next door and wondered if Louisa had ever set foot inside her neighbor's home.

"You want some coffee?" Juliet asked as they walked into the kitchen. The whole room would have benefited from a good scrubbing, so Jillian decided against eating or drinking anything.

"I had a cup not long ago," Jillian said. "If I have any more, my hands will shake. But you go ahead."

"Coffee doesn't bother me," Juliet said as she spooned instant coffee into a mug, then filled it with tap water. Jillian, used to Bertie's rich, fresh-brewed coffee, suppressed a shudder.

"I was impressed by your concern for Louisa," Jillian said.

Juliet paused in the process of putting her coffee mug in the microwave and eyed her suspiciously for a moment, but then her expression softened. "She was a nice person."

"I thought so too," Jillian said. "I worked with her in a program she put together to teach teens how to cook and bake. She really went above and beyond to help the kids succeed."

The microwave beeped and Juliet popped the door open. "She liked kids, I think."

"They liked her as well." Jillian assessed the seat of the closest kitchen chair. It didn't appear too grimy, so she sat down gingerly. "I was wondering: Do you know who visited Louisa on the last day she was home?"

The other woman's gaze sharpened, then quickly softened. She carried her coffee mug over and sat opposite Jillian. "I didn't see. It's not like I watched her house. I'm not nosy."

"Right," Jillian said. "But the houses are quite close together. I imagine looking out at your own lawn would mean you see a good bit of Louisa's house."

"That's true." Juliet blew across her coffee and slurped at it. Then she put the cup down on the dinette table. "There was a man who hung around Louisa's house. It was the same man I saw there at the hospital. I don't know his name. Kinda weaselly fella."

"Did you ever see Louisa and this man together?"

"No. I considered calling the police about him lurking. I thought he might be casing her place to burglarize it. I even told Louisa about it and asked her if she wanted me to call the cops the next time I saw him. She laughed it off. She said no one would bother stalking or robbing her because she didn't have anything worth taking. But she seemed really nervous after that."

"Did she suggest she knew the identity of the man at the time?"

"She said she hadn't seen anyone. She was nice, but not really chatty."

Jillian's gaze drifted to the wall clock. She needed to get back to the bakery before Bertie's appointment, and she said as much to Juliet.

"You can come by again if you want," Juliet said. "I liked Louisa. I feel really bad about what happened to her."

"We all do," Jillian agreed.

On the drive back to the bakery, she wondered if she'd actually learned anything at all. Apparently Patrick Hinkley had been lurking around Louisa's house, which was interesting and more than a little creepy. Since he'd already admitted to a romantic interest in her, Jillian supposed that could explain it. But she also had reason to believe his feelings were something other than affection, since he certainly didn't seem to be grieving over Louisa's death. There was Celia's report of Patrick weeping in his car—but that could have been guilt, couldn't it?

Jillian swung her car into a slot in front of The Chocolate Shoppe. She knew Bertie would fuss at her for it, but she hoped to slip out later and do some more poking into Louisa's affairs . . . as soon as she figured out which affair to poke.

She walked into the bakery and stopped with a sigh when she saw Gooder bent slightly and peering into the front display case. "I don't know why you're bothering to browse," Jillian said. "You're going to buy a bear claw. You always buy a bear claw."

Gooder grinned at her. "True, but I figure it's like going to an art museum. You might have your favorite painting, but it's a waste if you don't admire the others as well."

"I'll let my grandmother know you consider her an artist."

"She knows she's an artist." Gooder made a show of checking his watch. "I see you're just getting in. Off annoying the populace again, Miss Marple?"

Jillian folded her arms over her chest and ignored the question, offering one of her own instead. "Did you know Louisa Byrne had a stalker?"

He raised his eyebrows. "It's the first I heard of it. Do you know who it was?"

"Well, maybe 'stalker' is a little extreme. But her coworker, Patrick Hinkley, had a big-time crush on her," Jillian said. "He was also in her hospital room before she woke up for the last time."

"As were you."

"True, but I wasn't messing with her pillow."

A smirk slipped across his face. "You think some guy was going to suffocate her with a pillow in the hospital?"

"I don't know." Jillian held Gooder's gaze for a moment, then gave up. "Probably not. But Louisa's neighbor said he had been lurking around her house. And at the hospital, he told me that he was secretly in love with her. Granted, when I saw him later at the parks department office, he certainly wasn't acting like a man who had lost the love of his life."

Gooder shrugged. "People process grief in all sorts of ways."

"And they pretend in all kinds of ways too," Jillian said. "You know, I'm wondering if the missing money from Louisa's husband's embezzling is tied up with what happened to her."

"Tied up with a traffic accident?"

"It's not the accident that I'm wondering about," Jillian said. "It's Louisa's presence in the woods when she was supposedly away helping out a sister. Have you talked to the sister?"

Gooder harrumphed. "I haven't even found a sister. Listen, I'm considering all possibilities at this point, but I would appreciate it if you wouldn't do too much to muddy the waters of the investigation."

"An investigation you are barely doing, apparently." Jillian poked him in the arm with her finger. "Considering I had to tell you about Louisa's stalker."

"Fine," he snapped. "I better get back to it then. Don't want the official investigation lagging behind Jillian Green's brilliant detective work." With that, he stomped out of the bakery without his bear claw.

She almost felt guilty about that, but after all, Gooder should be out investigating the circumstances that had led to Louisa's death. The issue was whether he was bothering to look in the right places.

But then again, am I?

Once back in the bakery's kitchen, Jillian threw herself into work, as much for the sense of accomplishing something as to make up for leaving the job to Bertie and Lenora for the last couple of hours. Jillian was aware of her grandmother watching her as she flipped through the card file for the pumpkin tea bread recipe, the next item on the order list.

Finally, with recipe in hand, she faced Bertie. "Did you want something?"

"Did you settle anything?" Bertie asked.

"Not really." Jillian walked to the storeroom to get walnuts for the recipe, and her grandmother followed her.

"Then why did you come back so soon?" Bertie asked.

"You have a doctor's appointment."

"Not for another while yet. And I could put it off, besides. I need you settled. You're as scattered as those nuts are going to be if you don't watch how you pick up that sack. It's already been opened."

Jillian glanced at the resealable bag in her arms and saw she was holding it upside down, stressing the plastic zipper that held the contents in place. She carefully righted it. "I'm fine." She started to pass her grandmother, but Bertie caught her arm.

"I know I can be an old grouch, but I do care. What did you do this morning? What did you find out?"

"Not much." Shoulders sagging, Jillian went to one of the counters near Lenora in the kitchen and set the bag of walnuts down beside a mixer. As she gathered the rest of the ingredients, which were all close at hand, she told Bertie and

Lenora about her visits at Belmont Mansion and then with Louisa's neighbor. "I have puzzle pieces, but none of them fit together particularly well."

"Sounds to me like you ought to be paying attention to Louisa's stalker," Bertie said. "I don't trust a man who hangs around and stares."

Jillian almost laughed at Bertie's assessment, considering the octogenarian had inspired more than one man to skirt the issue instead of being direct. But Bertie was scary, and Jillian could fully understand why men would be hesitant to approach her. Louisa seemed a much less intimidating person. Which left the question: If Patrick actually liked Louisa, why not tell her?

"It's possible that Louisa had noticed his odd behavior and it bothered her," Jillian said. "The teens, her neighbor, and other coworkers all said she'd been increasingly nervous. But if it was Patrick who had worried her, why not confront him? Or take it to human resources?"

"Maybe she did confront Patrick," Bertie suggested. "She would probably have done that in private, and the only person who would know is him."

Jillian shoveled scoops of flour into the large bowl for the bread's dry ingredients. "I don't think he'd tell." She started to say something else, then closed her mouth into a tight line as she finished measuring the flour.

"Clearly you have a theory that is dying to come out," Bertie said. "Do tell."

"Actually, I have two theories." Jillian shifted the flour back to the shelf and grabbed the container of baking powder. "Right now, it sounds like Patrick Hinkley was obsessed with Louisa. He says he was in love with her, but he's not acting like a man who's grieving a lost love—well, other than a secondhand report that he cried in his car. One of his coworkers says he was miffed when

Louisa got the program director job that he wanted. So maybe he was watching for a chance to get her fired."

"And?" Bertie asked when Jillian paused.

"And maybe while searching for dirt on Louisa, he found out about her husband's embezzling. And maybe he found out the money was still missing. And maybe he decided all that money would be better than getting the program director job."

"That's a lot of maybes," Bertie said.

Jillian spooned baking soda into the bowl. "True, but Patrick was the person who reported Louisa's disappearance was a visit to her sister, which certainly appears to have been a lie. Unless her sister lives in a cave in the woods."

Lenora walked over to the cooler and came back with a container of fresh pumpkin. She plunked it on the counter. "You said you had two theories."

Jillian measured spices into the dry ingredients. "My other option is Rand McCall."

"That good-looking man you've been flirting with?" Lenora asked.

"I have not been flirting with him." Jillian tossed a spoonful of cinnamon into the bowl with enough force to create a small cloud, making them all cough.

"Fine." Bertie fanned her face. "You don't have to asphyxiate us to get your point across. What about this fellow?"

"He's recently out of jail. He spent the last few months in the same federal prison as Louisa's husband. Rand said he didn't recognize the man's name, but he could have lied. He might have learned of the missing money and come to Moss Hollow specifically to find it."

"And you think he saw Louisa as his means of doing that?" Bertie asked as she peeled the lid off the pumpkin and began measuring it.

"If he confronted Louisa, I could imagine her being scared. He's a big guy. He's been affable every time I've seen him, but that doesn't mean he doesn't have a darker side."

Bertie snapped the lid back on the pumpkin. "I suppose that makes as much sense as anything."

"Not quite," Jillian said. "Matthew says Rand has barely left the property since he got the job. If that's true, he wouldn't have had the opportunity to be involved with Louisa's disappearance. But Matthew is an old, sick man. He may not know what the gardener is up to all the time."

"It sounds to me like you have more questions than answers, but I have to go or I'll be late for my appointment." Bertie patted Jillian's hand. "Promise you'll try to focus on work. I'd like to come back to my bakery intact."

"I'll give it my best effort."

And she did, managing to shove the puzzles aside long enough to help Lenora fill the rest of the day's orders. They were already working on prep for Wednesday when Bertie came back, grumbling about waiting in cold doctor's offices for the opportunity to answer a lot of fool questions and be pointlessly poked and prodded.

"There is a point," Jillian said. "It's to keep you healthy. Speaking of which, did the doctor have anything to say about your health?"

"My health is fine." Clearly considering the case closed, Bertie put her hands on her hips and scrutinized the kitchen. "I see you've managed not to catch anything on fire."

Jillian rolled her eyes, wondering if she was ever going to live down her disastrous first weeks at the bakery. "I managed."

Bertie's glare softened. "You've actually become a good baker. I knew you had it in you. I believe I told you that on the phone when I lured you back here."

Jillian smiled at her. "I believe you did. And in that spirit, you didn't have any cupcakes on order for tomorrow. Don't you think we'll need some? We usually get a rush near the end of the week."

"Tomorrow's only Wednesday," Bertie said. "You just like frosting cupcakes. Bread is our big Wednesday seller." And from there, talk moved on to orders and prep until it was time to close the bakery and go home.

When Jillian pulled out of her parking space, she almost turned her car toward Belle Haven. She wasn't quite ready to call it a day on her investigation, though, so she circled the block and headed for Greyson & Sons. As the Nathan County coroner, Hunter might have information about Louisa that could help Jillian narrow in on one of the two men on her suspect list.

When she got to the funeral home, Oliver Kent met her at the door. "Was Mr. Greyson expecting you?" he asked. Oliver often sounded a little nervous, as though he thought Jillian might yell at him or create some kind of scene.

"No," Jillian said. "But I hoped he'd have a minute."

"I imagine he'll make one." Oliver stepped back from the door, making room for Jillian to walk into the foyer. He fidgeted with his glasses. He dropped his voice, as if they might be overheard in the empty room. "Mr. Greyson is with the deceased."

"Which deceased?" Jillian asked, speaking at a whisper equal to Oliver's.

Oliver's lips pressed into a moue of distaste. "The woman the police asked him to examine."

"Louisa Byrne?"

"I believe that is the deceased's name," Oliver said. "He is likely to be busy for the next few hours. Perhaps you could come again on a different day."

"I will be glad to do that if it's Hunter's preference. I'll tell you what. I'll head on back to Hunter's office and you go ask him if he has a minute to visit with me. If he wants, we can chat in his workroom."

Jillian saw a nerve jump in Oliver's face, making his right eye twitch. "Of course. You know the way to the office." He spun on his heel and walked away.

Jillian smiled after him. *That man's springs are wound a little too tight.* She walked to Hunter's office and let the relaxing decor soothe her while she waited.

When the office door opened a few minutes later, Hunter was clearly delighted to see her. He took both her hands as she rose from the office chair. "You smell like pumpkin spice," he said as he kissed her cheek.

"I suppose there are worse scents."

"I don't think I've smelled anything better recently." He took her hand and tugged her down to sit beside him in one of the two chairs that faced the desk. "Does this visit mean you'd like another impulsive date?"

Jillian sank into the chair that always seemed to mold itself to her. "I'd love one, but I should get home. I didn't tell Bertie I planned a detour, and she might worry. I mostly came by to get some insight into the case you're working on."

"Yes, Oliver told me he'd informed you of what I was doing," Hunter said. "The poor woman."

"Did you find anything that could explain why she was in the woods?"

Hunter's face clouded. "Jillian, this is a police investigation."

Jillian jumped on that, leaning forward eagerly. "So you did find something?"

He sighed. "She had a considerable number of bruises and scratches, including a partially healed cut on her arm. But then, she'd run through the woods in the dark. It would be shocking if she wasn't scratched up. And the truck caused the internal damage that eventually killed her."

The reference to the partially healed cut made Jillian sit up. She pointed to a spot on her own arm. "Was the cut about here?"

He nodded. "It didn't happen when the truck struck her. It showed signs of weeks of healing."

"She said that was a cat scratch."

Hunter shook his head. "It was a slice, probably from a knife. It wasn't large, but it would have left a scar. She really should have had it stitched up when it happened."

Jillian leaned back in the chair. "So something was happening even when I first met her. I keep coming back to the feeling that I should have done more. I could tell she was afraid of something when she was at the baking classes, that she needed help. I should have pushed. I should have made her let me help her." She gazed at her hands, doubt and guilt coursing through her.

"You can't force people to make wise decisions," Hunter said gently. Then a ghost of a smile tugged at the corner of his mouth. "Believe me, I've tried."

"Why do I get the feeling that comment was about me?" she asked.

The smile grew a bit, but then he sobered. "I shouldn't tell you this, but I know it's hardly going to stay secret after I submit my report. There were ligature marks on Louisa's wrists. At some point, she was tied up."

Jillian gasped. "That fits. I've been thinking that someone is after the whereabouts of her husband's embezzled money. That person could have kidnapped Louisa and taken her out to the woods—to get the information out of her where no one would disturb them."

"I suppose it's possible."

"I need to talk to Grange Oatley," Jillian said.

"The man in prison?"

"Right. He's central to all of this. I'm sure of it. If I can get him to tell me where he hid the money, we can use it to lure the kidnapper."

"No."

"I know," Jillian said. "He hasn't been willing to tell anyone in the past, but once he finds out that money is the reason his wife was killed, he may care enough to reveal the money's whereabouts."

Hunter leaned forward and took her hands again. "Jillian, you are not going to visit a men's prison."

She blinked at him. "I know it's likely going to be hard for me to get permission, but maybe with Laura Lee's help—"

"No," Hunter said. "I'm not talking about whether you could manage to finagle your way in there. I wouldn't be surprised if you figured out a way to chat up the president of the United States. I mean that you're not going to a federal prison because it's a bad, ridiculous, dangerous idea. I don't want you doing it."

She blinked at him, not sure she was hearing right.

"I know you don't like it," he said, his voice tight with strained patience, "but I'm putting my foot down."

"You're putting your foot down?" she echoed softly.

Hunter's jaw tightened. "Yes."

Jillian took several deep breaths. "I see. You seem to be confused. I'm not a child. Neither your foot nor any other part of you governs my behavior. I came to you for advice, support, and friendship, not control."

Hunter ran his hand through his hair, leaving it wildly askew. "That's not what I meant."

"Really? Because I'm not seeing another interpretation. We've run into this problem before. I know you don't like it when my desire to help gets me in trouble, and I love you for that concern, but it cannot turn into you giving me orders."

"I wasn't giving you an order," he said. "Not exactly."

Jillian stood up. "I appreciate you taking a break to talk to me. I do. But I think it would be best for both of us if we ended the conversation now. I'm going home. It's been a long day."

Hunter stood. "Jillian, we should talk this out."

She raised a hand. "No, I'm pretty sure that's exactly what we shouldn't do. Not right now. All we're going to do is make a bigger mess. Good night."

And with that, she marched out of the office. She expected to hear Hunter call after her, but the only thing that followed her out of the room was silence.

14

"You are a nincompoop!"

Jillian glared at her grandmother. "Have I told you lately how much I appreciate the unwavering support of my family?"

Bertie shook her finger at Jillian. "Don't get sassy with me, young lady."

Cornelia laid a placating hand on her sister's arm. "What Bertie is trying to say is that Hunter cares about you. He wants you to stay safe."

Jillian groaned. "I know that, but protecting me and controlling me are not the same thing."

"When you're afraid for someone," Cornelia said gently, "it can be hard to know the difference."

"Indeed."

The teakettle shrieked on the stove, making everyone jump. Bertie stomped off to the kitchen cupboards and began rooting through the tea, muttering about how Jillian was willing to listen to Cornelia but not her.

"I was listening to both of you," Jillian called after her. "But I'm still not okay with the whole 'putting my foot down' thing. Hunter's feet aren't in control of my decisions."

"I'm sure Hunter is going to realize that," Cornelia said. "He'll apologize, and you'll apologize, and everything will be fine."

"I'll apologize?" Jillian gave a derisive snort. "What will I apologize for?"

"Being a nincompoop," Bertie said.

Jillian chose to ignore that statement. She walked over and leaned on the kitchen counter. "Fine, then I'll wait for Hunter to come to his senses."

"In the meantime," Cornelia said, moving closer to Jillian with Possum at her feet, "you might want to examine your own motivation here." The cat meowed as if in agreement.

Bertie carried a mug over and set it in front of Jillian with a solid thump. "You can say that again."

Jillian looked into the mug, where a bag of chamomile tea floated in the hot water. "I don't know what you two are talking about."

"It seems to me that this situation with Louisa is hitting awfully close to home for you," her aunt said. "Considering your fiancé went to prison for embezzling."

Jillian reached over and grabbed the bear-shaped bottle of honey to cover her discomfort. "Ex-fiancé," she muttered.

"He wasn't an ex until after you found out about the embez-zling," Bertie reminded her. "Plus, with Savannah's wedding coming up, it seems to me that all this is likely to make you a little sensitive."

Jillian considered asking her grandmother if calling her a nincompoop was an appropriate way of responding to emotional distress and sensitivity, but she decided she was tired of arguing for one evening. "I honestly don't see those two things being connected."

Cornelia reached out and patted her arm. "Just be careful that you don't let fear ruin a good relationship."

Jillian took a sip of her tea. As much as she wanted to continue to defend her anger against Hunter, she knew Cornelia had a point. The whole situation was a little too familiar, and she did identify with Louisa. But she didn't see that as a reason *not* to find out what happened to the poor woman. "I'll think about it," she said finally.

Cornelia and Bertie let it drop and steered the conversation to Possum, mainly because Cornelia was carrying him around in the kitchen. "You know I'd rather you didn't do that," Bertie said. "It gives the floating cat hair too much advantage."

"I know, and normally I wouldn't," Cornelia said, which made Jillian choke on a swallow of tea. Cornelia carried the cat into the kitchen at least once a day. "But I'm concerned that Raymond is depressed."

Jillian looked up at the cat contentedly cuddled in her great-aunt's arms. "What makes you think he's depressed?"

"It was a message he sent me."

"The cat sent you a message?"

"Raymond sent me a message." Cornelia's tone was lofty. "I was laying out the tear-out cards to see if I could get some information that would help you in your investigation. And he jumped up on my bed, grabbed a card, and ran off with it. I had to reach under the highboy to get it back."

"And that made you think he was depressed," Bertie said flatly. "Instead of thinking he's a cat and they do things like that."

Cornelia narrowed her eyes at her sister. "It was a specific card with a specific message. It was the tear-out card for a psychology magazine, and the top story on the card was about depression. I'm sure Raymond was trying to tell me he was depressed."

"Maybe he was trying to tell you that you need a doctor," Bertie said.

This caused the discussion to devolve into sisterly sniping, and since Jillian had nothing of value to contribute about Possum's mental health, she carried her mug of tea to the breakfast nook and pulled out her phone. If anyone could get her in to see a prisoner, it would be Laura Lee.

"Forget it," her friend told her the moment she made the request. "It's not going to happen. You're crazy for asking."

"Well, I suppose that's better than being a nincompoop, which is what Bertie's been calling me tonight," Jillian said, which made her friend laugh. "I really think talking to him is the next step in finding out what really happened to Louisa."

"She was run over by a truck," Laura Lee said. "Really."

"You know what I'm talking about."

"I hate to be the voice of reason, but you'd never get in. It's not a hotel. It's not even a county jail. It's a federal prison. You're not Oatley's lawyer. You're not in law enforcement. You're not family. You've never even met the man, so there's no way you'd get on his list of approved visitors. There's no way for you to get in."

Jillian thought about that for a moment. "You're in law enforcement."

"I am."

"You could get in to see Oatley."

"If I had a legitimate reason. This isn't my case, Jillian. It's Gooder's case, so I'd have to ask him. Otherwise, it wouldn't go well for me."

"Will you try?"

"If I can think of an excuse that doesn't include your name."

"Attagirl," Jillian said brightly. "And when you do get to talk to him, find out if he knows a man named Rand McCall. He was in prison until recently, and now he's here working for Matthew Belmont."

"Poor man," Laura Lee said. "I wonder if he misses prison yet."

"Actually, they seem to be getting along. So you'll ask?"

"Yeah, if I can get the go-ahead from Gooder. But I might be able to find out about a relationship between Grange Oatley and McCall even if I don't go to the prison."

"How?" Jillian asked.

"I have my ways." Jillian could hear the smile in Laura Lee's voice. "I'll call you when and if I learn anything. Until then, try not to make Gooder mad. It'll only make this harder."

"I never *try* to make Gooder mad. Well, usually I'm not trying, but sometimes it's just fun," Jillian said, which made Laura Lee laugh again as she ended the call.

Jillian carried her mug to the sink and rinsed it out. Bertie and Cornelia had left the kitchen while Jillian was on the phone. *What I need is something to take my mind off everything.*

She followed the sound of a voice to the living room where Cornelia was seated in a cozy chair with Possum. A novel took up the small amount of space in her lap not being taken up by the cat.

"Were you talking to Possum?" Jillian asked.

"I was reading aloud," Cornelia said. "Raymond always loved Hercule Poirot, so I thought I'd read to him a little to raise his spirits." Possum blinked up at Jillian sleepily.

"Do you have book suggestions? I thought I might have a long, hot soak with a book."

"A few days ago I finished a wonderful Amish mystery. Well, it's not actually Amish since the main character owns an inn, but it has Amish people in it. Anyway, I liked it. You'll find the book in the library. I'm collecting all the books in the series."

"Thanks. I'll give it a try." Jillian left her great-aunt and wandered into the two-story library at Belle Haven, a cavernous room full of beautiful books and a never-ending supply of dust bunnies. She opened the door and stepped in, flipping the light switch. Unfortunately, the switch only turned on a few wall sconces instead of the brilliant overhead illumination Jillian would have preferred.

Her cell phone rang, nearly making Jillian jump out of her skin. She pressed her hand to her chest as she fished the phone out of her pocket and saw it was Gooder. *Laura Lee must not have been able to keep my name out of it.* "Don't be mad at Laura Lee," she said as soon as she answered the call.

"Huh?" Gooder said. "Why would I be mad at Laura Lee? What are you taking about?"

"Um, nothing. What are you calling about?"

"I'm down at the bakery. You'd better come down, and Bertie too. Someone has vandalized the front window, and I assume the message was for you."

"What message?" Jillian asked.

"It says, 'Mind your own business.' It's like they read my mind."

With a sinking heart, Jillian had to admit that did sound like it was probably directed at her. "I'll be right down."

When she relayed the message to Bertie, her grandmother raised an eyebrow. "I wonder who you've annoyed this time."

"I'm not sure, but clearly whoever kidnapped Louisa is feeling the pinch." Jillian looked at her grandmother, already in her pajamas and slippers. "I'll go to the bakery now on my own and sign any report papers. You don't need to come."

Bertie nodded. "You do that. Be sure to get everything documented. Take pictures. Who knows if we'll need to get the insurance company involved."

"I will." Jillian started to back out of her grandmother's room. "And I'm sorry."

"There's no call to be sorry for who you are. We'll sort it out. Now go talk to Gooder and try not to pick a fight."

Jillian was torn between being touched by her grandmother's initial supportive words and annoyed by two different people assuming her tiffs with Gooder were her fault. *He's the one who is always so judgmental and annoying.*

The sidewalk in front of the bakery had already grown a tidy collection of gawkers by the time Jillian found a parking place and trotted up the block to where a young deputy was snapping pictures of the bakery window while Gooder quizzed lookie-loos.

"Kind of you to join us, Miss Green," Gooder said.

"I came as soon as I told Bertie what happened. She's staying home."

"I don't blame her," Gooder said. "I wouldn't be here if I wasn't forced." He shivered. "I think a storm might be coming. The temperature has been dropping since I arrived."

Jillian walked over to study the dripping red paint on the window. The letters were messy and uneven, and the feathering along the edges of each letter suggested spray paint. "I want to try to get this off as soon as y'all are done taking pictures. I probably stand the best chance of doing it before the paint dries."

"I'd leave it be and take a razor blade to it after it dries," Gooder suggested. "You're just going to smear it around if you try now."

Jillian nearly asked Gooder what made him the spray-paint expert, but then she remembered that she was supposed to be trying to make nice. "Thanks for the suggestion."

Gooder's eyes widened in surprise.

Am I usually that crabby? Jillian wondered.

"Do you have any idea who might have done this?" Gooder asked.

"Someone associated with Louisa Byrne, I assume. I've been asking questions."

"Why?"

"Because she was kidnapped, and she died, and I knew her. Because I'm not sure enough people are asking questions."

"I meant 'Why am I not surprised?'" Gooder crossed his arms over his chest. "And by 'enough people,' I assume you mean me. Jillian, I only just heard about the ligature marks myself, which is what I assume you're referencing, since you're involved with our county coroner."

"Don't be making potshots at Hunter." Jillian glared at him.

"It's not Hunter Greyson I'd take a potshot at." Gooder bit off his words, then held up a hand. "Forget all that. Can you give me a list of the people you've talked to about Louisa?"

"Sure, but you have to know that with the Moss Hollow gossip network, it wouldn't have to be someone I actually talked to."

"So glad you're here to tell me how to do my job," he said sarcastically. "It'll give me a place to start, okay?"

Jillian rattled off a list of names and Gooder wrote them down.

"You know," he said as he finished writing the last name, "you probably should leave this alone while the damage is limited to a window in need of scraping. I really wouldn't want to see you get hurt." To Jillian's surprise, he sounded sincere.

"I'll try to be careful. Hey, did you ever learn anything useful about the gun from Louisa's fish tank?"

Gooder groaned. "You could at least pretend to take my advice. Fine. The gun had the serial number filed off, but when we sent it to the lab, they were able to restore a partial number. We haven't matched it to an owner yet. And the only trace evidence on it was from the tank. But it was a gun and when guns are involved, private citizens shouldn't be." He pointed his notepad at Jillian. "That means you."

"As far as we know, no gun has been used in this case," Jillian said. "It was just found in a tank with a bunch of poor dead fish."

Gooder huffed. "I still don't understand why someone cranked that tank heater up to full blast. The fish didn't stand a chance. But why kill fish? This whole thing is a confusing mess. And I most certainly don't like seeing this." He gestured at the vandalized window.

"It doesn't exactly brighten my day either." Jillian crossed her arms. "I get what you're saying about staying out of it, but now the investigation has come to my family's business. At this point, I'm not really likely to let it go."

Gooder harrumphed again. "Like you ever were. Fine. Your funeral."

With a chill, Jillian sincerely hoped that he didn't mean that literally.

On Wednesday, Jillian headed to work ahead of Bertie again. This time it was so she could get the message scraped off the front window before the bakery opened.

Lenora met her on the sidewalk with a bucket of water and a sponge. "When you get the paint scraped off, I'll wash off the bits and residue."

"How did you know I'd be here?" Jillian asked, pulling out a scraper with a razor blade she'd found in a toolbox at Belle Haven.

"I called Bertie to ask her what she wanted me to do about it, and she told me you were on your way." Lenora gestured toward the window. "I can't believe I slept through this last night. I went to bed early with a headache."

"Are you feeling okay now?" Jillian wondered if she should volunteer to take over the Wednesday night baking class, a thought that filled her with as much dread as the warning on the bakery window.

"I'm fine, honey. It started with a conversation I had on the phone with Dorie about their plans for Christmas. Sometimes the bullheadedness of that child leaves my head aching."

A smile tugged at Jillian's lips. She suspected she knew where Lenora's daughter had gotten her stubbornness. Lenora and her daughter clearly loved each other, but they knocked heads even more often than Jillian and Bertie.

With some vigorous scraping and sponging, they had the window mostly clean by the time Bertie unlocked the bakery door and leaned out. "Lenora, come on in and help me set up for the bread orders. Jillian can handle the rest."

Lenora handed over the bucket, and Jillian was left wondering why every vote of confidence her grandmother made involved giving Jillian more work.

A screech of brakes drew her attention away from the window. Celia and Sidney piled out of a small car that straddled two of the parking spots in front of the bakery. A thin teenage boy stayed behind the wheel of the car, peering at Jillian through wire-rimmed glasses.

"He can't park there like that," Jillian said. "And why aren't you two in school?"

"School doesn't start until eight," Celia said with an eye roll. "And Blake isn't going to stay there."

"We had to see you," Sidney said. "We found something."

Celia held a handful of crumpled papers in the air. "Evidence."

"Evidence?" Jillian echoed. "Of what?"

"Of guilt." Celia waved the papers emphatically. "We can prove Patrick Hinkley was out to get Louisa."

Jillian quickly shushed them. Making accusations in public could land both girls in trouble, no matter how much Jillian might be persuaded to agree with them. "What are you two talking about?"

"We were investigating," Celia said smugly.

"On television, detectives and spies are constantly finding clues in people's trash," Sidney added. "So we went through his."

"And we found these." Celia waved the papers again, which meant Jillian couldn't see what they were.

"And of course, these should never have been in the trash can in the first place," Sidney said with a sniff. "Paper should be recycled, not sent to a landfill. Recycling is important, and hardly anyone around here seems to take it seriously."

"We do," Celia protested. "My mom even rinses out the tuna cans." She wrinkled her nose. "Though I sort of wish she'd rinse the tuna right out. I could live the rest of my life with no tuna."

"I agree." Sidney made a face. "Gross."

Jillian got impatient and snatched the papers out of Celia's hand, garnering yelps of protest from both teens. She could see the pages were torn from a legal pad and covered with scrawled handwriting. She squinted as she tried to make sense of the terrible penmanship.

"We had trouble reading it too," Celia said. "Sidney tried to say it's because he writes in cursive, and we didn't get a lot of cursive teaching in school, but I can see you're having trouble too, and you're old, so I figure you had cursive writing back in your day."

Jillian glanced up. "Yeah, we wrote cursive with dip pens on dinosaurs. I assume you finally got through these since you're sure they're clues. What do they say?"

"They're love notes." Sidney pointed at the top page in Jillian's hand. "That one even has poetry. Really cheesy poetry. We figured they're practice love notes since he threw them away and all."

Celia crossed her arms over her chest. "He practiced a lot."

"And he is proof that practice doesn't always make perfect," Sidney added.

Jillian worked out a few of the lines on the page and realized the girls were right. The pages were clearly Patrick's attempts to declare a romantic interest in Louisa. Technically, she supposed they were evidence that what he had told her in the hospital was true. Unless he went home afterward and wrote them, thinking he ought to have evidence to support a romantic interest no one else seemed to have noticed. "This is interesting," she said finally. "But it's not proof of wrongdoing. Unless you read a threat on any of the pages."

Sidney's face fell. "No, no threats. Just grossness."

"They are proof," Celia said. "You read them. This guy sounds desperate. The man was a creeper, and he probably kidnapped Ms. Byrne and carted her off to the woods, thinking he'd make her fall for him. I saw that in a movie once."

"Do your parents not monitor your movie watching at all?"

Both girls rolled their eyes. "We're not children," Sidney said.

Jillian disagreed, but decided to keep that thought to herself. "Well, these are interesting, even if they aren't proof. I'll pass them along to the police. At least it might make them talk to Patrick."

"When you do"—Celia poked the pages with one finger—"you be sure to give us credit for finding them."

"Credit?" Jillian raised her eyebrows. "You want me to tell Deputy Jones that you guys were going through someone's trash? You know he'll tell your parents."

Celia and Sidney exchanged glances and Celia grimaced. "Yeah, maybe not."

"I'd be grounded for life," Sidney added. "Well, at least *you* know we contributed, Ms. Green."

"I do." Jillian gave a quick smile. "Thanks." She watched the girls trudge back to the car and leave, then leaned against the window and tried to read the messy papers.

The bakery door opened and Jillian looked up to find Lenora standing with her hands on her hips. "Was that Celia out here? Why isn't she at school?"

"She said she had plenty of time to get there." Jillian held up the pages. "And she wanted to bring me these. Apparently, she and Sidney found them. They're practice love notes written by Patrick Hinkley to Louisa Byrne."

Lenora narrowed her eyes. "And where did those girls find them?"

Jillian cleared her throat nervously. "In his trash, I believe."

"I knew it!" Lenora stamped a foot. "You're rubbing off on them. I can't believe you're encouraging things like this. Don't you remember how this kind of behavior nearly got them both killed once before?"

Jillian shook her head. "First, I did not encourage them.

Second, I have not forgotten. I specifically told them to leave the investigating to the police." *Although maybe I should have repeated that advice today.* "But I don't control those girls. I'm not sure anyone controls that particular pair."

Lenora grunted. "You best come on inside before your grandmother finds you loitering out here." She nodded toward the window. "You did a nice job cleaning up."

Jillian inclined her head. "Thank you." She followed Lenora into the bakery and was soon suited up in her requisite long white apron and pink hairnet. She picked up the clipboard and scanned the orders while part of her brain decided on what to do about the notes. She had stuffed them in her purse, but she could hardly just cart them around everywhere she went. She should take them to Gooder, of course, and she would. But she wasn't certain that was where she should go first.

"If you're waiting for something to jump out at you from the clipboard, I can assign you a task," Bertie said from behind her.

Jillian set the clipboard down. "Assign away."

"You're sounding chipper, considering someone threatened you last night."

"I've learned not to let threats get me down," Jillian said.

"That's probably wise, considering how often you get them." Bertie put her hands on her hips, which reminded Jillian of Lenora staring at her with the exact same stance outside. The two women had clearly been working together long enough to pick up one another's mannerisms. "It turns out you get to make those cupcakes you were so eager to do yesterday. The elementary school made an order for a few dozen with icing in fall colors."

"I'm on it." Before Jillian could head to the closest mixer, Bertie caught her arm.

"What are you going to do with those notes?"

"Wow, Lenora told on me fast."

"Only because I noticed you were acting distracted and I asked her what she knew about it. I hope whatever you're going to do, it's not going to get you further into trouble."

"I will eventually take them to Gooder, but I want to read them first. Their very existence certainly suggests he told me the truth at the hospital. And it explains his hanging around Louisa's house and the staring that Bree Weston described."

"But you're still suspicious," her grandmother finished for her.

"I am. He doesn't seem like a man grieving for a lost love."

"Grief affects different people in different ways," Bertie said. "I remember when your grandfather died. Some folks said nasty things because I didn't cry in public." She lifted her chin. "You might be right, maybe he isn't grieving, but don't assume that's the case just because you can't see it."

Jillian nodded. "Yes ma'am."

Bertie raised an eyebrow. "Then again, he might have thought professing some romantic interest would get him into Louisa's personal life, where she might tell him what happened to all that money."

"That would be devious."

"It's also unlikely. I'm beginning to think you're contagious. First you inspire those girls to paw through someone's trash, and now you've got me coming up with preposterous theories. I'm going to go work in the storeroom until I come to my senses. You get on those cupcakes now."

"I will." Jillian walked over to the nearest mixer and began laying out the ingredients for the cupcakes. She glanced up to find Lenora peering at her.

Lenora pointed a finger at her. "I fully expect you to stop encouraging my cousin."

"I'm not encouraging her!" Jillian protested, but Lenora had resumed her own work and begun humming to show how much she wasn't paying attention to Jillian's claims of innocence. Jillian narrowed her eyes and gave a disgruntled grumble, then returned to her cupcake project.

As she worked, her head swirled with thoughts about the notes. She was itching to find a quiet spot to read through them line by line, but she didn't want to get Bertie worked up by trying to take a break already. Maybe after the cupcakes were frosted she could grab a cup of coffee and a table out front to read over the pages. In the meanwhile, the cupcakes would certainly end up better if she stopped woolgathering. She made a concerted effort to clear her head and focus.

She did so well that she barely noticed the passage of time as she made the batter and got the cupcakes in the oven. She mixed up some more sugar cookies while the cupcakes baked since she could frost the cookies and the cupcakes at the same time when they were both cooled.

She was pulling both the cupcakes and the cookies from the oven when Maggie poked her head in from the front and inhaled deeply. "It smells great back here."

Jillian had to agree. The chocolate from the cupcakes and sweet scent of vanilla from the cookies made the kitchen smell homey and delicious. "Do you need something?"

"Not me, but you have a visitor who really wants to talk to you." Maggie disappeared through the doorway without telling Jillian specifically who was waiting for her.

Jillian assumed the visitor would be Gooder, probably with some report papers for her to sign about the vandalism. She wondered if she should go ahead and give him the notes, even though she hated to give them up before she'd had time to give them a close reading. She was still debating it as she walked out to the front of the shop.

But the man waiting for her on the other side of the counter wasn't Gooder. It was Hunter.

He gazed at her solemnly. His normally bright-blue eyes were shadowy. For the first time ever, Jillian thought that he looked like an undertaker, and her stomach clenched with nerves.

Was this the death of their relationship once and for all?

Jillian reached a hand to her head and swept away the hideous pink hairnet, smiling nervously at Hunter. "Hi."

"Can we talk?" he asked.

"Of course." Her voice was uneven. "Um, let me get you some coffee." She used the pouring of the coffee to hold off the emotions that threatened to swamp her. If he had come to break up with her over their disagreement, she was in no hurry to get the bad news.

With two coffee cups in hand, she started around the counter, then stopped. "Maybe I should get us something to eat. Do you want a bear claw? A doughnut?" She stood frozen, staring at Hunter and wanting to put off whatever he'd come to say.

Hunter reached out and took one of the cups of coffee, then took Jillian's hand. "I don't need anything to eat, but I would like to talk to you. Is that all right?"

She couldn't even stammer a response. She bobbed her head, wishing she had any idea how to hold off the moment when he broke up with her. He walked to the table farthest from the counter, the one customers often passed over because it was so close to the restroom. It was the one where she and Hunter always sat, as it offered the closest thing to privacy anyone could find in the small seating area. Jillian wondered if it was some kind of sign that their favorite table was the one near the bathroom.

Hunter pulled out her chair and Jillian sank down in it without speaking. He sat across from her, but his attention remained focused on his coffee. Jillian wanted to tell him that he didn't have to do this. They could work things out. But her throat felt closed, and she wasn't sure she could make a sound if she tried.

Finally, he made eye contact with her. "Jillian, I'm sorry."

She stared at him, wide-eyed and waiting for him to add whatever reason he had for breaking up with her. He reached out and took her hand, and she jolted at the contact, her nerves strung so tight she thought she might scream. Half of her wanted to make him stop talking and hold off the moment forever. The other half wanted him to get on with it and yank the bandage off.

"I know I have no right to dictate your behavior," he said. "You had every reason to be angry with me, but I hope you're not ready to give up on us."

She felt her breath hitch in her chest. *Is he not breaking up with me?*

"I'm not apologizing for caring about you," he said firmly. "And I can't even promise I won't ever get bossy again. You scare me so much sometimes. I can't imagine not having you around."

Jillian drew in slow breaths, surprised that her tight chest had loosened enough to allow it. He was apologizing. He wasn't calling it all off.

"I know what I said was wrong," he said. "But could you throw me a line here? If you're not ready to forgive me, will you at least consider it?"

"I forgive you," Jillian said, her voice sounding thin in her ears.

He studied her face for a moment. "I am not telling you what to do, but I can't help but ask. Please don't go to that prison."

"I'm not."

He sat back, surprise clear on his face. "You're not?"

"Apparently there's no way I could get a visitor's pass. The man doesn't know me, and I have no official tie to the case."

"So you would have gone," he said quietly.

"I was planning to, but honestly, I don't know." She offered him a weak smile. "I'd be scared to death to go someplace like that by myself. Anyway, Laura Lee is going to see what she can find out."

A slow grin spread across his face. "In that case, would you be free to go to dinner with me after work on Friday?"

Jillian suspected her own expression reflected the same relief. "I would be happy to."

As soon as she spoke, the entire bakery broke into applause. Her face burning with embarrassment, Jillian rolled her eyes. *Apparently our private table is anything but.*

Jillian decided to own the moment and stood to take a bow, making everyone laugh.

Hunter got to his feet as well. "I need to get back to work. I'm glad we're good."

"Me too."

Hunter leaned over and kissed her, prompting another round of applause. As he left, Jillian hurried back to the kitchen to avoid the teasing that she knew was inevitable. Both Bertie and Lenora seemed to be suspiciously busy, their gazes pointedly on their work, though grins lingered on both of their faces. Jillian considered telling them that they weren't fooling anyone. She figured they'd been watching from the kitchen so they couldn't have missed Hunter's kiss. She decided that if they wanted to pretend they hadn't been spying on her, then she'd go with it. At least she'd miss out on the teasing that way.

She grabbed a fresh hairnet and began stuffing her ponytail into it, feeling immensely lighter now that her relationship with Hunter felt right again. It had surprised her how scared she'd been when she thought he was breaking up with her. She had pushed him pretty far before with her investigating and the danger it put her in, but though she'd worried about their relationship, she'd never felt quite as bereft at the thought of losing him. *I'm falling in love*, she realized, then shook her head. *No. I might as well be honest. I've already fallen, and I've fallen hard.* The vulnerability that came with that was scary, but she couldn't help but smile all the same.

She let thoughts of Hunter carry her through the next several orders and even found herself humming. But eventually all the questions about Louisa Byrne snuck back in and nagged at her. What should her next move be? Surely there was something she could do that wasn't particularly dangerous, yet still yielded results. The obvious choice would be to follow the lead the girls had found. She needed to talk to Patrick Hinkley and ask him about the letters.

The chance to do so came at noon when Bertie shooed her out of the kitchen. "It's your lunch break. Go outside, breathe fresh air."

"Are you sure?" Jillian asked. "I could help you prep for the class tonight."

"The parks department called and said they were canceling the class tonight in light of Louisa's death."

Jillian frowned. "That doesn't make sense. They had Monday's class."

Bertie shrugged. "Honestly, I am relieved."

"I can understand that," Jillian said. "Okay, I'll be back in an hour." She was perfectly happy to get out of the bakery. She drove over to the parks department office, only to find the building was closed for their lunch hour. Jillian stood on the sidewalk, clutching the rumpled love notes and staring at the sign on the door. *What do I do now?*

She started back to her car, thinking maybe she'd treat herself to a sandwich somewhere. She was still on the sidewalk when she spotted Patrick Hinkley coming from around the other end of the building and heading for the lot. She quickly changed direction to head him off. "Mr. Hinkley?" she called.

He faced her, shielding his eyes from the sun. "Yes?" He blinked at her for a moment. "If this is about canceling the class tonight, I realized we probably appeared uncaring by not taking a brief break in light of Louisa's passing. We'll be back on Monday."

"Actually, I didn't come to ask about the class. I'd like to ask you about these." She held up the papers as she approached him.

He frowned at the rumpled pages. Once he saw them clearly and recognized his own handwriting, his puzzlement became anger. "Where did you get those?"

"Someone brought them to me. I believe they are yours."

"How dare you steal my property!"

"Actually, the people who brought them to me assured me they'd come from the garbage. Technically, garbage is no longer private property."

"So what is this? What do you want from me?"

"I'd like to know if these are real."

"What do you mean, 'real'?" he asked, his hostile glare giving way to confusion.

"Did you feel the way you say you did?"

He crossed his arms over his chest. "I already told you how I felt at the hospital in a moment of weakness. I see no reason to have this discussion."

"Why didn't you ever tell Louisa?" Jillian asked.

He sighed and let his arms drop. "I wanted to. I planned to. But I couldn't talk to her at work." He gestured toward the building. "That place is a nest of gossip. You should have heard them when people found out about Louisa's husband and the money."

Jillian widened her eyes. "So her coworkers knew about the missing money?"

"They certainly talked about it enough. It was ghoulish, and Louisa must have known. It's part of why she kept to herself so much, I'm sure of it." He stared across the parking lot. "And I never understood." He returned his gaze to Jillian, his expression intense. "How could that man have been so stupid? He had everything—a good job, an amazing wife, probably a nice home. They had no children, and they both worked. How much money did he feel like he needed?"

"I don't know." Jillian considered that a good question. With her own ex-fiancé, she'd asked that same thing over and over.

"So I couldn't talk to her at work. I went to her house a couple times, thinking I would tell her there. But she was so private. I didn't know if she'd simply be angry at me for invading her personal space, so I'd always talk myself out of it when I got there. Then I wrote those." He gestured toward the pages clutched in her hand. "But it felt wrong. That kind of thing should be done face to face. And I could never get the words right. If I couldn't get them right in a letter, how could I ever get them right while staring right at her?"

"So she didn't know," Jillian said softly.

"I don't think so. She never acted like she'd guessed." Patrick's voice grew ragged as he continued to speak. "I ask myself now if anything would have changed if I'd told her. If she'd felt the same way, and we were together, could I have kept her safe?" He broke down, weeping as he turned away from Jillian and stumbled toward his car. She let him go, not wanting to make things worse for him, though she doubted he was in fit shape to drive. To her relief, he simply sat in his car, the tinted window glass offering what Jillian hoped was a sense of privacy.

She walked back to her own car, the letters still in her hand. She was mildly surprised that he hadn't tried to get them back. She wasn't sure what to do with them. She no longer considered Patrick likely to have hurt Louisa. *Obsessed men have hurt women before*, a voice in the back of her mind nagged. With a groan, she stuffed the letters in her glove box. She wouldn't discard them, but she was definitely putting Patrick Hinkley on the back burner of her suspect list. *Which leaves me with what?*

She rested her forehead on the steering wheel. What could she do now? She doubted Patrick's guilt. She couldn't go quiz Louisa's husband about the money or about whether he knew Rand, but at least she had Laura Lee working on that question. *Am I ever going to figure out how Louisa ended up in the woods?* That thought sparked something in Jillian. She could try to track down where Louisa had spent her last days, beginning with where she'd spent some of her last minutes. She needed to go check out the spot where Louisa was hit.

She pulled her phone out of her pocket and stared down at it. She hated to bother Laura Lee since she'd already begged her for a favor relating to the investigation. Then she smiled as she thought back to the conversation at the Sweetie Pies meeting. Laura Lee wasn't the only friend who knew exactly where Louisa's accident had occurred.

Savannah answered the phone right away, her voice bright. "Do you think a peanut butter wedding cake would be weird? James is crazy about peanut butter."

"Not weird," Jillian said. "You should have whatever you want, but you might want to think about food allergies. Peanuts are a really common allergen these days, so you'd have to let people know."

"Oh yeah. I don't really want to include allergy warning signs in my wedding decor. James will have to pick something else."

"The top layer could be peanut butter," Jillian suggested. "If we're careful about cross contamination, that would work. The top layer is traditionally eaten by the two of you on your first wedding anniversary."

"I'll think about it. But I know you didn't call to hear me freak out about cake. What can I do for you?"

"I wondered if you might be free to tromp around in the woods with me tomorrow. I want to check out the area near where Louisa had her accident, and it sounds like you know the exact spot."

"The Lovers' Oak, you mean? I definitely know it. We can't park right there, though, because it's on a blind curve. That would be just asking for someone to smash your Prius to white confetti."

"I'll trust you to know the best place to park, since you've got the experience with the area. I suppose I should see if Maudie can give me directions to the cabin from there."

"No need," Savannah said. "I know where the cabin is."

"You do?"

Savannah laughed. "You think only men go hunting?"

"You went hunting?" Jillian was shocked. *Do I not know Savannah at all?*

Savannah laughed again. "No, I was just giving you a hard time. The old hunting cabin was also a popular couples' spot in high school. I never actually went there with a boy, but I did go see it. It didn't inspire romantic thoughts then, and I doubt it's gotten any nicer over the years."

"I'm glad you know where we're going. If we search the area from the road to the cabin, I'm sure we'll find something."

"Sounds like you're catching Cornelia's premonition thing."

"Hardly. I'm mostly working on wishful thinking, but I'm really wishful. I don't have any other line of investigation right now, and I'm going nuts with nothing to pursue. And this isn't dangerous, so it won't freak Hunter out. It's the best of all possible worlds."

"I don't know about it not being dangerous," Savannah said. "There are snakes in the woods. You'll want to wear boots."

Jillian shuddered at the thought of snakes. "Thanks for the tip."

They worked out the details for Jillian to pick Savannah up in the morning. Now all she had to do was convince Bertie to let her skip out on work. How hard could that be?

Jillian decided to wait until after work to talk to Bertie about taking Thursday morning off, so she threw herself into the list of orders and shook off all mental distractions. Bertie kept giving her piercing glances, clearly noticing the burst of intense industry, but she didn't ask any questions, so Jillian didn't volunteer any information.

That didn't mean she didn't volunteer at all. "I can stay and close today," she said when Bertie passed by her decorating station as Jillian finished piping roses on a birthday cake.

"You don't have plans with Hunter?" Bertie asked.

Jillian smiled. "I do, but they're for dinner on Friday."

"I heard the applause earlier," Bertie said, "but by the time Lenora and I got to the doorway, we'd missed the show. I don't suppose you have something to tell me?"

"About Hunter?"

Her grandmother put her hands on her hips and scowled. "Yes, about Hunter."

"We'd had a small disagreement, but we worked it out and we're going out to dinner Friday night."

"And people applauded that?"

Jillian dropped her gaze back to the cake in front of her. "I think sometimes people in Moss Hollow are hard up for entertainment."

Bertie grunted and kept her pointed gaze fixed on Jillian a few more moments before relaxing her scowl. "Thanks for staying. I was planning to do some inventory, but I can do that another time. I think I'll go home and put my feet up."

Jillian aimed a sunny smile at her. "Good idea."

Bertie's gaze was still a bit narrow, but she bobbed her head in another silent thanks and walked across the room to check the order list. Jillian knew her grandmother would never leave without making sure everything was in hand.

Jillian set her piping bag aside and picked up the cake order slip, checking on the spelling of the recipient's name before beginning to pipe the message. She'd learned to double- and even triple-check name spellings. It was no easy thing to erase a cake.

As she assembled a second piping bag with the writing tip, she saw Bertie walk out to the front to give Maggie last-minute instructions. As soon as her grandmother was out of the room, Lenora stepped over to the decorating station. "What's up with you?"

"Me?" Jillian asked. "What makes you think anything is up with me?"

"You're not acting normal."

"I'm working."

"That's what I mean. Ever since you got back from your little errand, you've been working like a house afire. No staring into space. No questions about Moss Hollow gossip. Just work."

Jillian frowned at Lenora before mixing some more food coloring into the bowl of dainty pink frosting she'd been using for the roses. She wanted the message on the cake to be a bit darker. "You make it sound like I'm usually a slacker."

"Not a slacker," Lenora said. "But not usually so fast and furious. And you didn't have one word to say about your mysterious errand, which isn't like you at all. You typically want to process those things out loud."

"Okay, fine." Jillian dropped her voice slightly. "I wanted to be sure to get a lot of work in this afternoon because I plan to take the morning off."

Lenora cocked her head and raised her eyebrows. "Does Bertie know that?"

"Does Bertie know what?" Bertie asked as she walked back into the kitchen.

"That Jillian is taking the morning off."

Thanks, Lenora. Jillian turned to her grandmother. "I was going to talk to you about it when I got home tonight."

"This is a business, not a jail. And you're a grown woman. You don't have to tiptoe around," Bertie said. "You doing something with Hunter? I thought your plans were for supper. Didn't you just tell me that?"

Jillian lowered her gaze to the frosting bowl and began whipping the color in. "My plans with Hunter are for supper, but after work on Friday. I need tomorrow morning off to do something with Savannah."

Bertie's expression lightened. Jillian knew her grandmother loved Savannah as if she were another granddaughter. It was like she never noticed that Savannah loved going on "adventures" with Jillian. "That early?"

"Well, not until it's light out." Even in the summer, they generally got to the bakery before sunrise, but in the fall it felt particularly dark when Jillian left for work in the mornings. "But it's still going to be early, so I probably won't come in until after I'm done with Savannah. If you need me to put in an hour or two I can, but I'd need to leave around the time we open."

"What will you two be up to?" Bertie asked.

Jillian slowed her rapid whisking of the frosting. *Might as well go for broke.* "I want to go out and check the area where Louisa was hit by the truck. Savannah knows the spot, so we're going to go check it out together. It's the only thing I could think of to get a fresh perspective."

"Sometimes your single-mindedness reminds me of your mother." Bertie sighed. "You know I don't like this. It pulls you away from things that actually are important: your work and Hunter."

"Louisa was important too," Jillian said quietly. She gently tapped the whisk against the frosting bowl, then set it aside. "And she doesn't get to go back to her work."

"And it's pointless to remind you that the police can handle whatever happened to Louisa," Bertie said. "Fine, go meet Savannah. But don't you get caught up in something that gets you in trouble with Hunter. If you aren't careful, you're going to lose him."

Jillian raised her gaze to lock eyes with Bertie. "If I lose Hunter by being too concerned about people, then I never had him in the first place." As she said the words, they rang true in her head. The Hunter Greyson she had fallen for cared about people. And that was something she didn't need to question. "Hunter understands. We talked, and we're good. I can't walk away from this. Maybe my experience in California with trusting an untrustworthy man, an embezzler, is getting wrapped up in how important this is to me, but it's not standing in my way with Hunter."

Lenora cleared her throat. "If you want my opinion—"

"Only if you agree with me," Bertie interrupted.

"I do and I don't," Lenora said. "Honestly, I'd like to see Jillian help get to the bottom of this fast. Celia has gotten wrapped up in this mess with her friend Sidney, and they're not going to let it go until it's solved. So the sooner Jillian sorts it out, the sooner those girls will be safe. I don't want them ending up in trouble they can't get out of."

"And I don't want that for Jillian either." Bertie put her hands on her hips.

Lenora gestured dismissively. "Jillian will make it through fine. She's always mucking around in things and coming out the other side without a scratch."

Jillian thought back to some of the situations she'd gotten into since returning to Georgia. She couldn't exactly say she never got a scratch.

Bertie raised her hands. "Fine. Go investigate. Try not to get yourself killed. And don't be getting Savannah killed either. That girl is about to get married."

Jillian wasn't sure she understood why Savannah's death needed to be particularly prevented close to her wedding, but she wasn't going to risk annoying Bertie—more than she already had anyway. "No getting killed. Check."

Bertie slipped her apron off. "You're lucky orders are lighter tomorrow. Now finish up that cake before the frosting gets hard."

"Yes ma'am."

Bertie muttered as she walked away, but Jillian could tell she wasn't really mad. *All things considered, that went pretty well.*

The next morning, Jillian rushed around trying to find her car key. With a house as big as Belle Haven, Jillian had learned to be organized about where she put things like keys, her purse, or her sunglasses, but somehow the keys weren't on her dresser when she woke up, even though she clearly remembered putting them there.

She was rifling through a pile of cooking magazines in the kitchen when Cornelia came in, Possum following at her heels. Jillian glanced up. "Have you seen my—" She stopped talking when Cornelia dropped her keys on the counter. "Why did you have my keys?"

"Raymond brought them to me this morning," Cornelia said. "I think he was trying to send a message."

"I assume the message is 'Tell Jillian not to leave the bedroom door open where the cat can get the car keys.'"

Cornelia gave her a long, pitying look. "It's a shame you're so insistent upon suppressing your sensitive nature. I'm certain you'd be open to the spirit realm if you'd let yourself."

"I'm open to enough weirdness," Jillian said. "And I have to run. I'm picking up Savannah."

Cornelia bent and scooped up the cat. "Be careful today. I'm certain Raymond took your keys for a reason."

Because they're shiny and they jingle. Jillian decided not to harass her great-aunt and instead gave her a peck on the cheek. "I'll be careful."

As soon as she trotted outside, Jillian was glad for the thick cotton sweater she'd chosen to wear with her jeans. The temperature had grown colder in the night, and a chilly breeze tossed her hair. She pulled her mane of red curls back into a ponytail with an elastic band as she walked to the Prius, hoping Savannah wouldn't be annoyed at her arriving late.

When she got to Savannah's house, she found her friend standing outside, leaning on the end of her Buick and tapping at her phone. Like Jillian, Savannah was dressed for the cool weather in a sweater knit from variegated yarn in shades of gold, green, and rust. The sweater matched the rust color of her slim-legged pants. Savannah's hair was tucked under a gold scarf, reminding Jillian of a movie star from the 1950s.

Jillian pulled in and hopped out. "I'm sorry I'm late. I hope you weren't getting ready to call me."

Savannah shook her head as she slipped the phone into her leather shoulder bag. "I was texting with James about potential dates for his bachelor party. He is doing a lot of pre-apologizing."

"Oh, does Hunter have something wild planned?" Jillian asked. As James's best man, Hunter was in charge of the bachelor party, but he hadn't mentioned any ideas to Jillian.

Savannah walked over to open the passenger door of Jillian's

Prius. "I doubt it, knowing your boyfriend, but James doesn't know. He's covering his bases."

"Smart man."

Savannah gave her a sunny smile. "That's why I'm marrying him."

On the drive out to the country, Savannah and Jillian chatted about the upcoming wedding. "Are you nervous?" Jillian asked. "I'd be in a panic."

"About the wedding?"

"About being married." Jillian's fingers tightened on the wheel. "Honestly, there is nothing Bertie or Cornelia would like better than to see me married, but I don't know if I'm really the marrying kind. Maybe I'm better off as the dating kind."

Savannah laughed. "You're going to be an interesting bride-to-be someday." She stretched out her legs as much as the small car allowed. "I'm not worried about being married. I've spent a lot of years knowing James was the one for me."

"I hope it's every bit as perfect as you're thinking," Jillian said, cutting a side glance at her friend.

Again, Savannah laughed. "I don't expect it to be perfect. No relationship is. I expect it to be an adventure, and I love adventure, even when it's scary or challenging."

"And Bertie thinks you're the levelheaded one."

When they reached the old tree that was their only landmark for Louisa's accident, they took a moment to admire the huge oak. "I'm surprised the poor thing is still alive," Jillian said as she ran her finger over a freshly carved name, one of dozens she could see. "Apparently Moss Hollow teens are still carving the names of their beloveds into the trunk."

"Look here." Savannah pointed to one of the thick branches hanging low. Jillian saw the thin crooked letters. *James.* "That one's mine."

"Did he dream of you?"

She shrugged. "Likely not, considering he went ahead and married Nadine. But I remember coming out here in the dark all alone. The woods were full of sounds. It was scary and exciting."

"An adventure," Jillian said.

"Yup, and now it's time for another one. Louisa must have come out over there." They crossed the road and started into the woods. There was no sign of Louisa's passage that Jillian could see, and she wished they had Laura Lee with them. Their friend was definitely a more skilled tracker.

"I guess we should head for the cabin," Jillian said. "Maybe we'll run across some evidence between here and there."

Most of the walk was long and prickly, with plenty of uneven ground and roots catching at Jillian's feet. She was reminded why she didn't spend a lot of time walking in the woods. "Laura Lee was right. It's a long way from the cabin to the road where Louisa came out. And I can't see a person running far or fast on this terrain."

"We're nearly to the hardest part." Savannah pointed ahead. "There's some old barbed-wire fencing. I heard that at one time it was to keep hunters off a piece of private land, but whoever put it up hasn't taken care of it."

"Can we get past it?" Jillian asked.

"Sure."

When they reached the fence, Savannah stomped down on the loose, rusty wire with her thick boots to push it toward the ground so Jillian could step over. Once she was over, Savannah joined her. "Easy-peasy."

"In the daylight," Jillian agreed. "But what about at night?" She began walking along beside the wire for a few feet. "Savannah, check this out!" In a tangle of wire between two thin pine trees, a scrap of cloth hung on the wire. They hurried closer and discovered the cloth was stained. "Is that blood?"

"I don't know," Savannah said. "Do you think we should take it with us?"

"Yes, but first we need to take photos of it in place." Jillian pulled out her phone and began snapping shots of the fence and the cloth. "We won't know if this came from Louisa's clothes until we give it to Laura Lee."

Savannah pulled an envelope and a pair of tweezers from her leather bag. "True, but I think we'll find it is. The fence is pretty easy to see in the daylight, and not too many people go walking in these woods at night." She tugged the cloth from the fence wire and dropped it in the envelope, then gestured up ahead. "We're almost to the cabin."

They walked the rest of the way faster, the discovery of the cloth lending some energy to their steps. Jillian grew increasingly sure that the cabin would turn out to be Louisa's starting point on the night she'd been hit by the truck.

The rough-board cabin was as shabby as Jillian had expected. In fact, the whole structure leaned slightly to one side. Jillian pushed open the poorly hung door and gaped around. The cabin was one big room with a floor made up of the same kind of rough-sawn wood as the outside of the building. The only piece of furniture inside was a ladder-back chair that lay broken on the floor. Hanks of rope and scraps of duct tape lay in the dust around the chair. Jillian tugged Savannah into the room. "This is it. This is where someone held Louisa."

Savannah hung back. "It certainly appears that way. We should stay out and call the sheriff's department. This is definitely something they need to handle."

Jillian pulled her phone out of her pocket. "I don't have any reception here. How about you?"

Savannah retrieved her own phone from her bag and shook her head. "We'll have to head back to the road. I know I had reception there."

"Okay, let me get some photos and we'll go." Jillian's heart pounded in her chest as she snapped the photos, being careful not to venture too far into the room and mess up potential evidence. She knew now where Louisa had been before she was hit by the truck. The evidence in the room, added to what Hunter had found on the body, made it clear that someone had kidnapped Louisa and brought her here. Now they needed to figure out why, and Jillian suspected the answer to that lay with Grange Oatley.

As soon as she was done taking the photos, they traipsed back through the woods. When they got to the barbed-wire fence, Savannah stomped it down again, but this time it slipped from under the toe of Savannah's boot as Jillian stepped over and she tripped, landing sprawling in the leaves. At that exact moment, a sharp crack rang out and something bit into the bark of the tree close to where Jillian had been a moment before.

"Someone's shooting!" Savannah threw herself to the ground next to Jillian.

Another shot rang out, hitting the tree again. Someone had declared open season on Jillian and Savannah.

Jillian and Savannah scrambled out of the brush until they were able to run through the trees, trying to stay low. Either the thick undergrowth frustrated the shooter too much or else he lost interest, as no more shots rang out.

When they got to the road, Jillian finally had enough reception to call Laura Lee. She put her on speakerphone and gasped out a recap of their discovery at the cabin and the shooting.

"Where are you right now?" Laura Lee asked. "Are you safe?"

"We're at the road, walking back to my car," Jillian said. "There haven't been any shots for a while."

"That could be because the shooter was hoping for a clear shot, which he could certainly have now with you two on the road. Use the woods for cover until you reach the car. I'm on my way."

Jillian and Savannah exchanged glances, then dashed for the woods on the opposite side of the road from where they'd been shot at. They lost the phone signal almost immediately, but it didn't matter. Laura Lee was on her way.

When they reached the Prius, they paused, peering around a tree at the car for a minute. "You know," Jillian said, "it occurs to me that the best place to wait to pick us off is at the car. I mean, the shooter has to know we'd come back here."

Savannah nodded. "I'm okay with waiting for Laura Lee right behind this tree."

"So tell me: How is the adventure going for you?"

That actually made Savannah laugh, and she clamped a hand over her mouth. After a moment, she moved her hand aside and whispered, "I'm enjoying the adrenaline rush."

"You're a strange woman," Jillian whispered back. "But I'm glad you're my friend."

Several minutes later, a sheriff's department car pulled up and Laura Lee got out. She glanced around, worry on her face. When Jillian and Savannah dashed out of the woods, relief flooded the young deputy's expression.

"Any more shots fired?" Laura Lee asked.

"No," Jillian said, panting slightly as she reached the road. "But we thought it was better to be safe than sorry."

"Smart. I imagine the shooter is long gone now. You guys want to show me your discoveries?"

Jillian glanced nervously at the woods across the road. "I've lost my enthusiasm for tromping through the forest. There are things you need to see, though."

With Savannah leading the way, they walked back into the woods. Jillian was impressed with the skill her friend showed in guiding them back to the cabin in exactly the same path they'd taken. Granted, the brush was considerably more broken and disturbed after the two of them had crashed through it while fleeing the shooter.

When they reached the spot where the shots had torn at the bark of an old pine, Laura Lee tied a cloth to the tree to mark it. "I've got a tech coming. We'll look for the bullets and maybe some spent cartridges if she can find where the shooter was standing."

A chill ran through Jillian at Laura Lee's casual mention of "the shooter," and she rubbed her arms. It wasn't the first time she'd been shot at, but Jillian could never get comfortable with the idea that someone was willing to hurt her, maybe even kill her. And the fact that it was a different person every time was positively depressing. *Maybe Bertie is right. I need to reevaluate my choices.*

"You know, this might not have had anything to do with you guys," Laura Lee said. "It's entirely possible it was someone out shooting in the woods because they're an idiot. There are plenty of idiots with guns around."

Jillian dropped her hands from her arms. "I might believe that if they hadn't nearly hit us twice."

"Fair enough. We'll see what the tech finds. Now, let's check out the cabin. On the phone you said you guys found proof Louisa was there?"

"This way," Savannah said, enthusiasm ringing in her voice.

Jillian wanted to go home, have some hot tea, and curl into a shaking ball, but if Savannah and Laura Lee were so cheerfully enthusiastic, she wasn't going to be the wimpy one. "Might as well get it over with."

"We have one more thing to show you first, Laura Lee. We found it on the barbed wire fence." Savannah pulled the envelope holding the fabric scrap from her bag and handed it to Laura Lee. "We would have left it where we found it, but we were afraid the kidnapper might come back to clean up and take it."

"We think there's blood on it," Jillian added.

Laura Lee peeked into the envelope and frowned. "You may be right. It also matches the shirt Louisa was wearing when she was hit. I've seen it in evidence." She slipped the envelope into her pocket. Her face was slightly less enthusiastic as she said, "Let's head to the cabin."

A few minutes later, Jillian and Savannah stood in the doorway of the derelict shack as Laura Lee took a few careful steps in.

"Ropes and duct tape," Jillian said, pointing. "That plus the signs of restraint Hunter found on Louisa's body adds up to this being the place she was held."

"It's certainly indicating that," Laura Lee agreed. "Again, we'll have to wait to see what the tech learns. With this much rope and tape, I'm assuming there will be DNA evidence."

"I hope so," Savannah said.

The deputy squatted a few feet from the broken chair. "She probably turned the chair over while she was in it. Breaking the chair might be how she got away."

"That means she must have been here alone," Jillian said. "Otherwise, whoever tied her up would have stopped her."

"A reasonable theory. What's that?" Laura Lee gestured into a corner where the shadows were deeper.

"What's what?" Jillian squinted and saw something glinting faintly in the shadows.

Laura Lee carefully skirted the broken chair and made it to the corner. She pulled out her phone and snapped some photos, then used a pen from her pocket to hook the object on the ground. "Either of you recognize these?" She held up a pair of wire-frame glasses.

"They look like the ones Louisa wore," Jillian said.

"Apparently we won't be wanting for evidence." Laura Lee walked back to the door.

"You know what this means," Jillian said. "Louisa was kidnapped. And it has to be related to the money her husband stole. You've got to get me in to see Grange." She winced at the last sentence, feeling like she'd betrayed Hunter.

Laura Lee shook her head. "That's not possible. However, I made a trip out to the prison yesterday afternoon."

Jillian and Savannah both gaped at their friend. "And you didn't tell us?" Savannah demanded.

"It seemed like both of you almost getting shot was the lead story today," the deputy said drily. "And I'm telling you now."

"Did he say anything useful?" Jillian asked.

Laura Lee shoved her hands into the pockets of her sheriff's department jacket. "I showed him pictures of Louisa taken at the hospital, and he broke down. I guess he isn't exactly heartless. He confessed to stealing the money. Don't get too excited—I wasn't recording, and just hearing it won't carry any weight legally."

"Did he tell you where he hid the money?" Jillian asked.

Laura Lee's voice turned somber. "He didn't hide it. His mom was sick. Really sick. And the medical bills were going to make her lose her home. He stole the money and paid off all her bills, but he did it secretly. He didn't want anyone to know because he was worried that they'd somehow take the money back and leave his mom destitute again. He didn't even tell Louisa what he was doing."

"Wow," Savannah whispered.

"Yeah, he was pretty torn up to know that saving his mother may have killed his wife," Laura Lee said.

"So someone kidnapped Louisa to find money that didn't even exist?" Jillian asked in little more than a whisper.

"I don't think we should make that common knowledge," Laura Lee said. "We have a kidnapper and probably attempted murderer out there. The money could be bait to catch him."

"I could say I found it," Jillian said. "Everyone knows I'm poking around. It's Moss Hollow gossip fodder. What if I pretended I found it and was planning to keep it? It would certainly help out at the bakery and the mansion to get a whole lot of cash."

"No one would believe you'd steal a bunch of money." Savannah gave a derisive snort. "Or that Bertie would let you."

"Criminals tend to think everyone is dishonest, so it doesn't matter that most people won't believe it," Laura Lee said. "The kidnapper almost certainly would. But that would put you right in the center of the bull's-eye, Jillian."

"I've been there before." Jillian tried her best to sound braver than she felt.

B_y Friday morning, Bertie was barely speaking to Jillian except to express her complete contempt for the plan. She wasn't too happy with Laura Lee or Savannah either. "I thought those two had better sense."

"I'm not wild about the idea," Jillian protested, "but someone tried to shoot Savannah and me in the woods. We need to settle this."

Bertie slapped marmalade on a slice of toast so hard the bread broke in two. She tossed the pieces on her plate. "Fine. But I don't see how that requires you putting yourself in harm's way."

"Someone is after the embezzled money, so it's the only bait we have."

"This is a frightfully bad idea," Cornelia murmured. She'd been uncharacteristically quiet when Jillian had described the plan the night before. Now she poked morosely at a plate of cold scrambled eggs. "I did a dozen readings of the tear-out cards about this last night. All were terrifying."

In Jillian's opinion, the only scary thing about her great-aunt's readings was that she took them seriously. "I'm going to stay out of trouble. Laura Lee will be protecting me the whole time once we get the word out. It'll be a carefully monitored situation."

"Which sounds fine until we hold it up against your history of risky plans," Bertie said. "How often have they gone awry, hmm?"

"I believe the answer to that is, 'Every time,'" Cornelia said, in rare agreement with her sister.

"I'll be fine. And in the end, I'll be able to turn my full attention back to the bakery. Isn't that what you want?"

"At the moment, I'm less concerned about your attention than your safety," Bertie said. "Obviously I can't do anything to suppress this crazy idea, so just be careful. I don't like it."

Jillian gave a nod. "Duly noted. I'll come in with you this morning, but then I have to make trips out to get this story spread around. I need to be certain the prime suspects hear it."

Bertie grunted. "Whispering it to a few customers at the bakery and swearing them to secrecy should get it all over Moss Hollow by lunchtime."

"Probably, but I have to make sure two specific people hear it. I'll need to run a couple gossip errands this morning. But after that, I'll be back to work."

"While waiting for the bad guy to attack you," Bertie said. "That should be fun."

Cornelia swished the tea in her cup around. "This doesn't look good."

Bertie leaned over and peered into the cup. "It looks disgusting. You need to go back to tea bags like normal people."

"Don't you see it?" Cornelia shoved the tea cup at Jillian. "A gun. It's clearly a gun."

Jillian peeked into the cup. It was clearly a wad of wet tea leaves. "I promise to be careful of guns, Aunt Cornelia." She patted the woman's hand, but Cornelia pulled back the teacup, clearly not happy.

The prep hours at the bakery weren't much cheerier. Jillian spotted Bertie and Lenora whispering in the corner for quite some time. After that, neither of them spoke to her much, though she kept catching them staring at her dolefully. *This is going to be fun.*

She was actually relieved by midmorning when she could leave the bakery and put the plan in motion. She started with the parks department. Even though she no longer considered Patrick Hinkley a serious suspect, she couldn't be entirely certain.

Carrying a large bakery box stuffed with muffins, she pasted a smile on her face as she pushed open the door. She held the box up as the receptionist peered at her questioningly. "I know it's been a rough time for everyone here lately," Jillian said. "So I thought I'd bring a gift." She opened the lid of the box to show off the contents. "Pumpkin muffins."

"Well, isn't that nice," the woman said. "You go right on in with that." She paused, then added, "Though I don't suppose I could have one?"

Jillian smiled brightly at her. "Of course. Don't forget a napkin."

The receptionist beamed, and Jillian was soon in the large room where the staff worked in glum quiet. They all perked up when Jillian announced her gift, and soon the bakery box was surrounded.

The workers chatted quietly, but it was apparently enough noise to bring a scowling Patrick Hinkley from his office. "What's going on out here?"

Everyone froze, looking nervously toward their new boss. "Jillian brought muffins," Bree said. "They're excellent."

His expression softened slightly, and he walked over to examine the contents of the box. He raised his gaze to meet Jillian's. "How kind."

"I'm happy to do it. I know everyone is missing Louisa terribly."

Pain flashed in his eyes. "That's very generous."

"Not really. The bakery has come into an unexpected windfall. With our woes behind us, I thought it would be nice to spread the cheer."

"Oh?" His interest sounded feigned.

"Yes. Sometimes the curious cat lucks out. You just have to keep digging."

"That's nice I suppose," he said.

Jillian noticed that virtually every person in the room looked more interested in what she'd said than Patrick did. If he was after Louisa's money, he was either an amazing actor or awfully dense. Bree, on the other hand, stared at Jillian wide-eyed. "Did you find . . . ?" She let her voice trail off.

"I'm constantly finding things, especially hidden ones." It was clear Bree knew what she was hinting at, so she suspected the young woman would spread the story in the office as soon as Jillian left. "Well, I should get back to work. It was nice seeing all of you."

"Thank you, again," Patrick said, and this time his voice had a little more sincerity. Jillian gave him a big smile and left.

Her second box of muffins was headed to Belmont Mansion. Jillian was much more suspicious of Rand than of Patrick. Rand had been in prison with Louisa's ex. Sure, he claimed not to know the man, but Jillian couldn't expect the man to say, "Oh, yeah. He told me all about the money, so I thought I'd come out and force his wife to give me the cash."

When she carried the box of muffins to the front door, Allie opened it before she'd even rung the bell. "I was near a window when you pulled up," the young woman said with a giggle at Jillian's surprised expression. "Did you come to see me?"

"I came to bring a present." Jillian held up the box as an idea dawned on her. "And ask you for a favor."

Allie's eyes sparkled. "Sure, anything. Come in. Mr. Belmont is taking a nap so I have a little time to chat." She motioned for Jillian to follow her, and they walked the winding mansion halls to the kitchen.

"A nap?" Jillian echoed. "Already? It's not even lunchtime."

"He had kind of a bad night. Sometimes he's in pain."

Suddenly, Jillian felt guilty. She didn't like Matthew Belmont. He was a scheming, grumpy man whose daughters had grown up to be just as conniving, but she knew it must be hard for someone with such a strong personality to face the failing of his body. Her thoughts turned to Bertie. Jillian knew being in Matthew's situation would be horrible for her grandmother. "I'm sorry," she said softly.

"Don't be. It makes him mad when people feel sorry for him," Allie said as they reached the kitchen. "You want some coffee to go with the muffins?"

"I'd better not." Jillian put the box of muffins on the counter. "I've had a couple of cups already this morning. Any more and I'll have the jitters."

"Okay, then. What favor do you need?"

"It's about Rand. Do you think you could share some gossip with him for me?"

"I guess. He comes in for lunch every day, and we talk a little. It's mostly about plants, which I know nothing about, so gossip would be a nice change of pace. Besides, he likes you." Allie grinned. "He's asked about you."

Jillian raised her eyebrows. She knew Allie was assuming a romantic interest, but it could easily be the activity of a man keeping tabs on everyone, hoping to find the money. "I'm perfectly happy with Hunter."

"Oh, I know. But it's fun when good-looking guys are interested, right?"

"I suppose." She knew she was putting a damper on Allie's friendly teasing and gave the younger woman a smile. "The gossip I want you to tell Rand is that I found some money while investigating Louisa's murder. A lot of money."

Allie's eyes opened wide. "Did you?"

Jillian hated to lie to the friendly young woman, but she wasn't sure how good of an actress Allie would be if she knew the truth. She gave a conspiratorial wink. "That's the gossip."

Allie bounced on her toes and gave Jillian a quick hug. "Congratulations. I know you'll put it to good use." Then she took a muffin from the box and raised it like a wineglass. "To your success."

Guilt jabbed Jillian painfully but she smiled back. "Thanks, Allie."

By the time she got back to the bakery, Jillian was awash with guilt. She hoped the plan would end up bearing fruit because she hated lying to nice people. As she entered the kitchen, she noticed Bertie and Lenora weren't any cheerier than when she left.

"You're both still mad at me?" she asked.

"We're not mad," Lenora said. "We're worried. This scheme seems a little harebrained."

"I know. Bertie already scolded me about it."

"Not enough, apparently," Bertie grumbled. "But we've done our part. Maggie has been whispering to select customers about the bakery coming into a mysterious windfall. She's adding that the whole thing feels sketchy and maybe not even legal. I hope this works, because it's not doing our reputations any good."

Jillian had come in through the back door, so she hadn't seen the customers. She walked toward the doorway to the front. "You think it's hurting business?"

"Not exactly," Bertie said.

Jillian peeked out surreptitiously. The customer area was packed. Every table was full, and the line reached the door. Maggie was bustling between cash register, coffee maker, and display case.

"I'd tell you to go out and help, but that might cause a riot," Bertie said. "Come and tackle the orders so Lenora can go help wait on customers."

"Me?" Lenora didn't sound thrilled with the assignment.

"You're the only person who can claim ignorance and be believed," Bertie said. "And if we don't get Maggie some help, she's going to quit. So go work the front until Celia gets here."

Lenora grumbled but followed Bertie's directions. Jillian tackled the order list, working as efficiently as she could to try to make up for the chaos she'd caused. She worked through lunch, not daring to suggest another break.

Just about the time her stomach started growling, Lenora came back into the kitchen with Hunter in tow. "Can we talk?" he asked Jillian.

"I brought him back here because there's no way you two could have a private chat out there with the wolves. You take him on up to my apartment." She tossed Jillian the keys.

Jillian glanced at Bertie. "Don't be silly," her grandmother said. "Go."

Jillian led Hunter up to Lenora's small, neat apartment. Not wanting to sit on Lenora's living room furniture in her flour-coated work clothes, Jillian walked into the kitchen and gestured toward one of the vinyl dinette chairs. "Shall we sit?"

"We can," he said.

Jillian peered at his face nervously as they sat. He clearly wasn't happy. "You heard the gossip," she prompted.

"I did. And since I know you wouldn't get money in some nefarious way, I could smell one of your schemes."

"Actually, it was mostly Laura Lee's scheme," Jillian said. "Though I went along with it, of course."

"Of course you did. You're bait, I assume?"

"Something like that." Jillian explained about the trip to the cabin that she'd made with Savannah. She considered leaving out the part about being shot at, but it seemed unwise. He'd hear it eventually and then be doubly upset that she hadn't told him right away. The more she talked, the less his expression gave away. Finally, her story trailed off.

Hunter didn't say anything for a while, so Jillian asked, "Is this where you break up with me?"

A frown creased his brow. "I'm not going to break up with you. If I could throw away our relationship that lightly, I wouldn't be so worried in the first place. This plan certainly wouldn't be my first choice, but I see where it came from. And it seems that you would have continued to be in danger regardless of your actions. So I see only one clear option."

"Which is?"

"I'm going to make sure you don't spend one moment alone until the kidnapper is caught. And if you hear from Louisa's kidnapper, trying to arrange some kind of meeting, you've got to promise to tell me before you go haring off."

"I promise," Jillian said.

He glanced around the apartment. "Should I stay here until you get off work?"

A slow smile spread across her face. "I don't think I need a bodyguard at the bakery. There are a lot of people here. I promise not to leave until the end of the day."

"Fair enough. I'll pick you up for dinner here."

"I won't be ready for going out." She gestured to her grimy clothes. "I'll need to go home to change and shower. You can meet me there."

He shook his head. "I'll drive you home and wait. I haven't had a chance to visit with Cornelia in a while, and that's always interesting."

Jillian felt the slightest twinge of bullheadedness at Hunter bossing her around, but she suspected that now was not the time to exercise that particular personality trait. She smiled and nodded. "That'll be nice. Thank you. But I have my car here."

"I'll follow you home, then."

"That's not—" The word "necessary" caught in her throat at his expression. Jillian realized this situation was pushing Hunter to his limits and pushing their relationship onto rocky ground.

She didn't see how she could change anything now, but she had to hope they could survive it. With a weak smile, she nodded.

"Try not to get killed before work is over," Hunter said as he stood.

"I always try," Jillian said, intending her remark to be a joke, but she felt a small shiver of worry. *I hope this doesn't turn out to be the death of me. Or us.*

After Hunter left, Jillian assumed she was done being scolded for her plan. She was wrong. When Celia came in to work, she had Sidney in tow, and they both made a beeline into the kitchen. "Everybody out there is talking about how you're a thief!" Celia yelled, waving her hands.

Lenora set down the tray of éclairs she had just finished filling. "Celia Ryan," she said, "you lower your voice or march right out of this kitchen."

Celia chose the former. "How could you do something like that?"

"I told Celia that the gossip had to be wrong," Sidney whispered fiercely, her eyes shining. "I told her you wouldn't steal anything."

"And I told her about all the bills here and at Belle Haven," Celia said.

"What do you know about bills?" Lenora asked.

"I know my daddy says those big plantation houses suck up money like it's water in the middle of the desert," Celia said. "And he says this is just a bakery. How much money can y'all really get out of it?"

"Your daddy needs to remember that little pitchers have big ears," Lenora said.

Jillian desperately wanted to tell the girls about the plan so they wouldn't think ill of her. She glanced at Lenora, who gave one shake of her head. Jillian had to agree. They couldn't risk word getting out that this wasn't real. Instead, Jillian looked away from the girls. "I have work to do."

"I told you," Celia said to Sidney. "And now I'm going to tell

183

you, Miss Jillian Green. I'm not working for someone who would take advantage of what happened to Ms. Byrne. She was nice." She spun on her heel and marched out of the kitchen with Sidney trailing her, a forlorn expression on her face.

"I know you didn't like doing that," Lenora said. "But Celia can't keep a secret to save her life. And knowing would put them in danger."

"I know." Jillian's voice was weak.

Lenora carried her pan of éclairs over and put them on a shelf of a tall rolling cart. "Plus, it won't hurt for those two to stop idolizing you. Maybe they'll give up their detective games and stay out of trouble." She pushed the cart out to the front of the bakery where the crowd remained steady.

Though Jillian felt a pang at the glee Lenora seemed to have at the idea of Jillian losing her teen fans, she knew Lenora was right. Admiring her put them in danger. It was better if they despised her. *Better, but seriously painful.*

By late afternoon, Jillian was about tired of the sly looks she got every time she carried a tray to the front, or the not-so-quiet mutterings of "thief." Eventually, she stopped carrying anything out and let Lenora handle it.

She was painting an apple pie with egg wash when Maggie walked into the kitchen, holding an envelope. "A kid raced in and gave me this. It has your name on it." She peered curiously at the envelope as Jillian took it.

"Did you recognize the kid?"

Maggie nodded. "It was Mitch Doogan's son. That boy is wilder than a hare." She pointed a finger at the envelope. "It doesn't have any return address."

"So I see," Jillian said distractedly.

"Who's out watching the front?" Bertie called from where she stood at the ovens.

Maggie squeaked and hurried back to her post.

Jillian stared at the envelope for a moment. Her name was written in precise block letters, but, as Maggie had noticed, there were no other markings on the envelope.

"Open it already," Bertie said.

Jillian opened it carefully and pulled out a folded sheet of paper from inside. The print on this page had been done by computer, with no hints about the origin. The letter was short, giving a place and time to drop the money, well after dark. The final sentence made Jillian's hands shake.

Come alone or end up like Louisa.

"Well," she whispered, "it looks like the plan is on."

"Please don't get yourself killed," her grandmother said.

"I'll do my best not to." Jillian walked to the bakery office and called Laura Lee so they could work out the details. Jillian ended by telling the deputy that Maggie had recognized the boy. "She said it was Mitch Doogan's son."

"Sounds likely," Laura Lee said. "That boy is always up to make money, especially if it doesn't involve actual work. I'll go track him down and see if he can tell me who gave him the note. We might be able to head this off early."

"That would be nice," Jillian said. "But catching the guy in the act seems like a better idea."

"It won't hurt to go in knowing who it is we're up against. Are you okay? You sound funny."

"It's been a stressful day. Turns out I don't actually enjoy playing a thief."

"Once we get this settled, you can go back to being the hero."

That brought a bark of laughter from Jillian. "The best I normally get in the gossip mill is being called a busybody who lucks into answers. But I'm growing fonder of that designation."

Laura Lee offered a few more cheery words before they ended the call. Jillian went back to the order sheet, hoping to find something to occupy her mind and her nerves. By closing time, they'd filled all the orders, and Jillian had resorted to cleaning to keep her mind busy.

She was under one of the tables wiping down the legs when Hunter entered the kitchen. He looked down at Jillian, his eyebrows raised.

"I ran out of things to do," she said. "And we don't spend enough time cleaning the table legs."

"I see." He smiled at her. "Can I help?" He started to squat down, but Jillian quickly scooted out from under the table and shook her head.

"No need. We can go. I could really use a shower."

They left the bakery. As they walked toward their cars, Hunter took notice of Jillian's fidgeting. "Are you all right?"

Jillian admitted that she'd gotten the note and outlined the plan for later that evening. "I won't be alone," she said. "Laura Lee will be there the whole time."

"Perhaps I should come," Hunter said.

"I think an armed deputy will likely be enough. More people means more opportunities for the bad guy to realize it's a trap."

"I suppose," Hunter said as they reached his Lexus, which he'd parked next to Jillian's Prius. He opened her car door for her, then said, "Drive safe. I'll meet you at Belle Haven."

When they got to the mansion, Cornelia met them in the foyer, Possum at her feet. "Thank goodness you're here," she said. "I've received a warning from Raymond."

"Possum talking to you again?" Jillian asked before she could stop herself. She felt a small stab of guilt. She knew Cornelia didn't really believe the cat talked, but somehow Jillian always felt the need to make some effort to break through Cornelia's delusions about Possum. Or maybe she was just trying to distance herself from the lunacy. Either way, it was probably a little mean.

Cornelia ignored the question. "I was sharing an afternoon snack with Raymond." She shifted attention to include Hunter in the conversation. "Raymond appreciates a little bacon in the afternoon."

"Possum is going to end up looking like a furry basketball if you keep sneaking him human food," Jillian said. "Dr. West said he's getting tubby."

"He is not 'tubby,'" Cornelia insisted. "He's thickly muscled."

Jillian rolled her eyes, and Hunter reached out to rub Possum's head. "So how did you get this message?" he asked.

Cornelia turned to direct her story only to Hunter. "I was bending down to give Raymond a snack when he batted it out of my hand with his paw. When the bacon hit the floor, he batted it again and it slipped under the fridge."

Jillian groaned. "Did you get it? You know that will draw mice."

Cornelia ignored her. "Since Raymond is normally quite dexterous, I knew that was a message."

"A message?" Hunter wore a smile, but he was clearly confused. Like Jillian, he couldn't see a message in that.

"Of course. Raymond was trying to tell me that even a good thing can go sideways, and if you're not careful, all will be lost."

Jillian felt a chill at her great-aunt's words, then shook it off. "An interesting message, but I'll go get the broom, and we can make sure that at least Possum's bacon isn't lost."

"Make fun," Cornelia said. "But be careful. I don't know what's ahead for you, but it could all go terribly, horribly wrong."

After Cornelia's warning, the tension between Jillian and Hunter grew. Jillian barely touched her supper even though they went to Crazy Fish Bar & Grille, which was one of their favorites. Instead of eating, they carried on a fierce conversation in whispers to avoid being overheard by any of the tables around them. "Of course I'm coming," Hunter said as his salmon cooled on his plate.

"Having more people there increases our chances of blowing the whole thing." Jillian sipped her iced tea, hoping the sweet beverage would help cool her temper. It didn't. "I thought we had this settled. You can't have changed your mind because of Cornelia's warning. The woman thinks the cat is my great-uncle."

"I'm not confused," Hunter replied, his whisper suddenly calm. "But I know that Cornelia's warning came from her instinct to protect you. She knows you're in danger. So do I."

Jillian could feel the resolution behind Hunter's serene exterior so she stopped arguing. Instead she pulled out her phone. "Then I should text Laura Lee and warn her that I'm bringing an audience."

Hunter didn't rise to the bait in her tone. He merely popped a forkful of salmon into his mouth. Jillian saw him react to the cold fish and almost smiled. *Serves him right.*

Jillian turned her full attention to her phone to send the text. She got an immediate answer, but it wasn't a text, it was a call. Jillian made a face. "Laura Lee," she told Hunter. "She's not going to be happy about you coming along."

"Too bad."

But Laura Lee didn't seem fazed by it. "Try to get him to stay in the car though. The less we stress the kidnapper, the better. Plus, I'd prefer fewer people in the line of fire."

"You're expecting fire?" Jillian's voice was a squeak.

"Not expecting. Prepared for. By the way, I talked to the kid. He said some guy gave him the paper."

"What did the guy look like?" Jillian asked.

"According to the kid, he was an 'old guy.' But when I asked him to pick out someone about the same age, he said it was an old guy like Deputy Jones or Sheriff Henderson."

"The sheriff is nearly twice Gooder's age," Jillian said.

"Yeah, so the kid wasn't exactly helpful. At least we know it was a man. I don't know about you, but I'm feeling more informed."

Jillian groaned. "Personally, I'm feeling a little sick."

"Buck up," Laura Lee said cheerfully. "It'll all be over soon."

Jillian ended the call thinking that sounded far more ominous than Laura Lee had intended.

After their unpleasant dinner, Hunter drove her to the edge of town, where a barn listed painfully to one side. The night breeze whistled through the holes in the old building and the whole atmosphere was terrifying. Hunter pulled off the road a little way from the barn. "I don't see Laura Lee."

"I think that's the idea," Jillian said. "You're not supposed to see her." She reached down between her legs where a canvas bag lay. Before they'd left Belle Haven, Jillian had dug the bag out of the third-floor storage area and packed it with newspapers to give it enough weight to make it believably full of money.

"Maybe I should come with you."

"You've come with me far enough. We've already deviated from the instructions in the note. I'm hoping it won't make a difference."

Hunter didn't respond, and Jillian got out. Though she stumbled a few times in the dark, she managed to get to the door of the old barn without falling down. The note hadn't mentioned going inside, so she didn't. She stood in the darkness and shivered, wishing she'd chosen a heavier jacket. In her imagination, she pictured Laura Lee with night-vision goggles and a rifle, ready to blast anyone who might show up to hurt Jillian.

Time stretched long and cold, and Jillian jumped every time the breeze rustled leaves or small critters in the barn scurried behind her. None of the sounds turned out to be the kidnapper.

She stood in the cold for a full two hours, but no one showed up. Finally, Hunter walked up to her and wrapped a coat around Jillian. "No one is coming. Come and get warmed up."

"What went wrong?" Jillian asked, her lips trembling with cold.

"I don't know. Laura Lee called, telling us to meet her. Come on."

He drove a few yards down the road and steered onto a dirt road that looked like little more than a game trail. Jillian winced as tree limbs dragged against Hunter's beautiful car, but she saw no sign that it bothered him at all. They pulled into a clearing, where a sheriff's car already sat.

Hunter parked a few feet from the cruiser, then he and Jillian hopped out. Laura Lee joined them between the two vehicles.

"What happened?" Jillian asked.

"I have no idea," Laura Lee said. "Something spooked them, I guess."

"Hunter's car, maybe. It was obvious I didn't come alone," Jillian said grumpily.

"I can't apologize for that," Hunter said. "I'm not leaving you to whatever this person might do." He addressed Laura Lee. "So, what's next? Jillian lives in fear for her life from now on? Because I have to say, I won't accept that."

"I don't know," Laura Lee said. "But I have to assume this guy isn't going to give up on the money. We will hear from him."

Hunter wrapped an arm around Jillian. "Until then, I'm not leaving you alone."

Jillian was disappointed and scared, and the whole wad of emotions churned into anger. She fought the impulse to shrug his hand off her shoulder. "If you'd left me alone this time, we might be done with all this."

"You don't know that," he said.

"You're right. At this point, I don't know much." She looked to Laura Lee. "I'm going home, okay?"

The deputy shrugged. "I can't think of anything better to do."

Jillian whirled around and strode to Hunter's car, then simmered as he drove her to Belle Haven. She'd expected this whole thing to be over, but it wasn't.

Maybe Hunter and everyone else were right. Maybe this plan wasn't the wisest thing she'd ever done, but if Hunter had let her go through with it her way, they might have the kidnapper in custody. It might be over.

Hunter made a few attempts at conversation as they drove, but she barely responded. Instead, she found herself getting more and more irritated as time wore on. As they started up the driveway, Jillian was suddenly desperate to get away from him before she blew up completely. The second he pulled the car to a stop in front of the mansion, she swung open the door. "Good night."

"I thought I'd come in," he said.

"I think we've had enough time together for one night."

His face was all shadows despite the light shining from above the front door. "Jillian, I don't want to fight."

"I don't want to either. Which is why you should go. I'm going to have a long, hot bath and go to bed. Good night." She knew her tone was a little too harsh, and she suspected she wasn't being fair, but she was still cold and more than a little scared, so she didn't care. She slammed the car door and headed up the front stairs as she heard Hunter's car retreat back down the driveway.

When Jillian flung open the door, she was surprised to see all the lights on, even down the hall toward the kitchen. She pulled out her phone to check the time. It was getting late, and neither Cornelia nor Bertie was a night owl. *They must have been worried about me.*

"Don't worry," she called as she headed for the kitchen, where she expected to find her great-aunt and grandmother sipping herbal tea. "I'm fine. Nothing happened."

"That's because it was all happening here," Bertie said as Jillian stepped into the room.

Jillian froze, shock making it suddenly hard to breathe. Bertie and Cornelia were seated on straight-backed chairs dragged in from the dining room, and they were duct-taped in place.

Juliet Ward stood beside them, and she was pointing a rifle at Jillian. Behind her lurked an older man that Jillian didn't recognize, and he seemed completely miserable.

"Surprise," Juliet said with an unpleasant smile. "Time to give us the money." She elbowed the older man. "Go get that bag she's holding, Ben."

Ben hurried over and grabbed the canvas bag from Jillian's hand. She stared at him, recognizing the name. "Ben? You ran over Louisa."

"Not on purpose," he said. He handed the bag to Juliet, who balanced the rifle on her hip to accept it.

Juliet scoffed. "He was supposed to come and help me look for her, but she ran out in front of his truck. Ben's an idiot and a rotten driver, but he's the only brother I have."

"You gave the note to the boy," Jillian said. *Apparently "old guy" was a better description than Laura Lee thought.*

Ben nodded, his expression tense and miserable.

Juliet held the bag in one hand and the rifle in the other, clearly unsure how to check the contents of the bag and keep the gun on Jillian at the same time. Jillian was fairly sure things weren't going to improve when the woman saw the contents of the bag. Desperate to stall until she could come up with an idea of what to do, Jillian asked, "So how did you know about the money in the first place? Did Louisa trust you with that secret?"

"Hardly." Juliet rolled her eyes. "She was a cold fish, for sure. But I already knew about the money. I worked at the same company as Grange Oatley, right up until they blamed me for not noticing the disappearing money quickly enough and fired me. It drove me crazy that Grange got away with all that money and I got the short end of the stick. I figured his wife had it, but no one knew where she'd gone."

"How did you find out?"

"Luck. I lost my apartment. It's hard to pay for a place in the city with no job, so I came here to stay with my brother. Wouldn't you know it—I spotted Louisa Oatley. Of course, she was using a different name, but I recognized her right away. I used the last bit of money I had to rent the house next door and played the part of the sweet neighbor, but she didn't want a sweet neighbor. So I had to get serious."

"Serious how?"

Ben grunted, and Jillian glanced at him, but he didn't say anything else.

Juliet gave him a disgusted glare. "I sent Ben to scare the information out of Louisa with my handgun. But my idiot brother isn't good at menacing. Louisa took the gun away from him, and he had to use a kitchen knife to ward her off. Then he ran away. I thought she'd call the police for sure, but she didn't make a sound."

Jillian realized that experience was probably where Louisa got the wound on her arm, not to mention what made her so jumpy. She knew someone was out to get information she couldn't give. No wonder she was scared. *If she'd told me, maybe I could have helped.*

"A fish tank is an odd place to keep a gun," Jillian said finally, not really knowing what else to say. She had to keep Juliet from seeing the newspapers in the bag.

"She had it on the shelf of the fish tank stand. She went after it the night I came to get her. She nearly got it too. We wrestled for it, and she would have probably won, but she clearly doesn't like to hurt people. I personally don't mind." Juliet grinned and the smile made Jillian's skin crawl. "When I slugged her, she dropped the gun in the fish tank." The woman shuddered. "You can get diseases from animals. I wasn't putting my hand in there. But I saw an opportunity. I cranked up the heat on it and told her if I could do that to her fish, imagine what I'd do to everyone else she cared about if she didn't come with me. Then I dragged her out of there and out to the cabin so we could talk. I was going to go back for the gun when I had time, but that didn't work out so well."

"Louisa must have told you she didn't have any money."

"Yeah, she tried giving me that line. I would have gotten the truth out of her eventually, but I couldn't stay out there all the time, even after I made Louisa call that stalker from her work to tell him she was going out of town. It got him out of the way, but then I had to keep an eye on you. You were poking into everything and you wouldn't stop, not even when I made Louisa call you. And while I was out one night, Louisa got loose."

"But she didn't get away."

"No. Not that Ben was much help." Juliet thrust the gun at him. "Here. Hold this on her. I want to look at the money."

Here it comes.

Sure enough, Juliet ripped open the bag and screeched, "Where is it?"

"There isn't any," Jillian said. "Louisa was telling you the truth. Grange embezzled the money to pay off his mother's medical bills."

"Liar!" Juliet screamed. She threw the bag across the room and grabbed the gun from her brother. She shoved the barrel against Cornelia's chest. "You tell me where the money is, or you're going to be short one little old lady."

"Get that gun away from my sister!" Bertie hollered.

A yowl cut through the air. From somewhere in the house, Possum was making a horrific noise. Juliet shouted at Jillian, but it was difficult to hear her over the sound of the cat. The yowling went on and on.

With the rifle trained on Jillian, Juliet stomped over to the knife block and grabbed a long chef's blade. She took it to her brother. "Go and shut that cat up."

"No!" Cornelia shrieked.

"Shut up!" Juliet screamed at her. Ben hurried out of the room, and Jillian said a silent prayer for Possum.

"Okay, okay. I'll take you to the money," Jillian said. "I hid it in our tobacco barn. We had it renovated, and there's a lot of storage out there, so that's where I put it. My grandmother and aunt didn't know."

The cat's yowling ended abruptly, and Juliet smiled coldly. "Great. Show me. Now."

Jillian knew things would get even worse when they got to the barn and found nothing, but at least she'd have the woman and the gun well away from Bertie and Cornelia, and she'd keep it away from them or die trying.

She led Juliet out through the French doors opening off the living room. They crossed the long backyard and entered the gardens. "How far is this barn?" Juliet demanded.

"Not too far, just far enough to keep the money hidden."

Each time she stumbled over a tree root or stone in the darkness, Juliet cursed. Jillian half expected to be shot in the back at any moment simply from the woman falling over her own feet.

"That's the barn," Jillian said finally, gesturing toward the building looming blacker against the darkness. "We have electricity in there, so you'll be able to see once we get inside."

"Good."

As Jillian stepped into the clearing where the old barn sat, something smacked her ankles, knocking her to the ground. At the same moment, a tree limb whistled through the air where Jillian had been only moments before. It struck Juliet hard. The rifle fired, but the bullet passed safely by since Jillian was sprawled on the ground. From the sound, the rifle shot struck the side of the barn.

Laura Lee tackled Juliet, wrestling the gun away from her and knocking her to the ground, then rolling her over to cuff her. Hunter stepped out of the bushes next to Jillian and held out his hand. "I'm sorry I tripped you," he said. "I had to get you out of the path of the tree branch and any possible bullets. Are you hurt?"

Jillian took his hand and let him haul her to her feet. "No, I'm fine." Then her eyes widened. "We have to get back to the house. Ben attacked Possum, and he's in there with Bertie and Aunt Cornelia."

"Old Ben is in cuffs in my car," Laura Lee said. "The cat is fine, though it may be awhile before he forgives me for pulling his tail. I had to get Ben and this one separated before we could safely capture them. I'd hoped the one with the gun would come and check out the noise, but it all turned out okay."

"How did you know to come here?" Jillian asked.

"I couldn't leave you," Hunter said. "I was too worried. So I pulled down the drive and walked back."

"But not before calling me and insisting I put someone on the house," Laura Lee said. "I was already on my way out here. I wasn't comfortable with leaving y'all unguarded and figured I'd come and have an unofficial sleepover." She grinned. "You know, it's a good thing Hunter doesn't take 'buzz off' for an answer."

"I didn't tell him to buzz off," Jillian said defensively.

"Maybe not in those words." Laura Lee hauled Juliet to her feet. "I'll take Juliet here for a reunion with her brother."

"Thanks for the rescue," Jillian said.

"No problem." Laura Lee nodded toward Hunter. "You know, you should at least kiss the hero."

Juliet made a retching noise. "Can I be taken to jail now? You people make me sick."

"Happy to oblige," Laura Lee said. She winked at Jillian and guided the woman back up the trail toward the house.

"We'd best go inside," Jillian said to Hunter. "I'm sure Bertie and Cornelia are tired of sitting around."

"Sure." He took her hand.

She smiled at him a bit shyly. "Thanks for coming back."

"You had me scared half out of my mind," he said. "I was sure you weren't safe, but I was afraid you wouldn't let me protect you."

"You saved my life."

Hunter put his arms around her. "That's because I couldn't imagine mine without you in it. I love you, Jillian Green. And I'd say that even if Laura Lee was still here. I'd say it in front of anyone."

"I appreciate that." Jillian's skin flushed in the cold night air, and she knew it was those precious words that warmed her. "But I prefer to do this without an audience." She stood up on her toes and said, "I love you too." And then she kissed him.

Off to a Bad Tart
Book Eighteen Recipe

Savannah's Chocolate Scotchies
Ingredients

2 cups flour
⅔ cup unsweetened cocoa
 powder
¾ teaspoon baking soda
⅛ teaspoon salt
½ cup butter, softened
½ cup margarine, softened

1½ cups sugar
2 eggs
1½ teaspoons vanilla
1 cup butterscotch chips
1 cup semisweet chocolate
 chips

Directions

1. Preheat oven to 350 degrees.

2. In medium bowl, sift together flour, cocoa, baking soda, and salt. Set aside.

3. In large bowl, beat butter, margarine, sugar, eggs, and vanilla until light and fluffy. Stir in dry ingredients until well blended. Mix in the butterscotch and chocolate chips.

4. Drop dough by rounded tablespoonfuls onto ungreased cookie sheets.

5. Bake 8 to 10 minutes in preheated oven, or just until set. Cool slightly on the cookie sheets before transferring to wire racks to cool completely.